ISLAND

ALSO BY

JOHANNA SKIBSRUD

FICTION

The Sentimentalists

This Will Be Difficult to Explain and Other Stories

Quartet for the End of Time

Tiger, Tiger

POETRY

Late Nights with Wild Cowboys

I Do Not Think That I Could Love a Human Being

The Description of the World

CHILDREN

Sometimes We Think You Are a Monkey

ISLAND

Johanna Skibsrud

HAMISH HAMILTON
an imprint of Penguin Canada, a division of Penguin Random House Canada Limited

Canada • USA • UK • Ireland • Australia • New Zealand • India • South Africa • China

First published 2019

www.penguinrandomhouse.ca

LIBRARY AND ARCHIVES CANADA CATALOGUING IN PUBLICATION
Title: Island / Johanna Skibsrud.
Names: Skibsrud, Johanna, 1980- author.
Identifiers: Canadiana (print) 2019009950X | Canadiana (ebook) 20190099518 | ISBN 9780735234581 (hardcover) | ISBN 9780735234598 (HTML)
Classification: LCC PS8587.K46 I85 2019 | DDC C813/.54—dc23

Cover and book design by Jennifer Griffiths
Cover and interior images: (flowers and vines; spider; fly) courtesy of the Biodiversity Heritage Library; (paper texture) *Laon (Aisne)*, 1896, Gift of S.F. Joseph, Brussels, Rijksmuseum

Printed and bound in Canada

10 9 8 7 6 5 4 3 2 1

Penguin Random House
HAMISH HAMILTON CANADA

Islands scars of the water
Islands evidence of wounds

—*AIMÉ CÉSAIRE,*
Notebook of a Return
to the Native Land

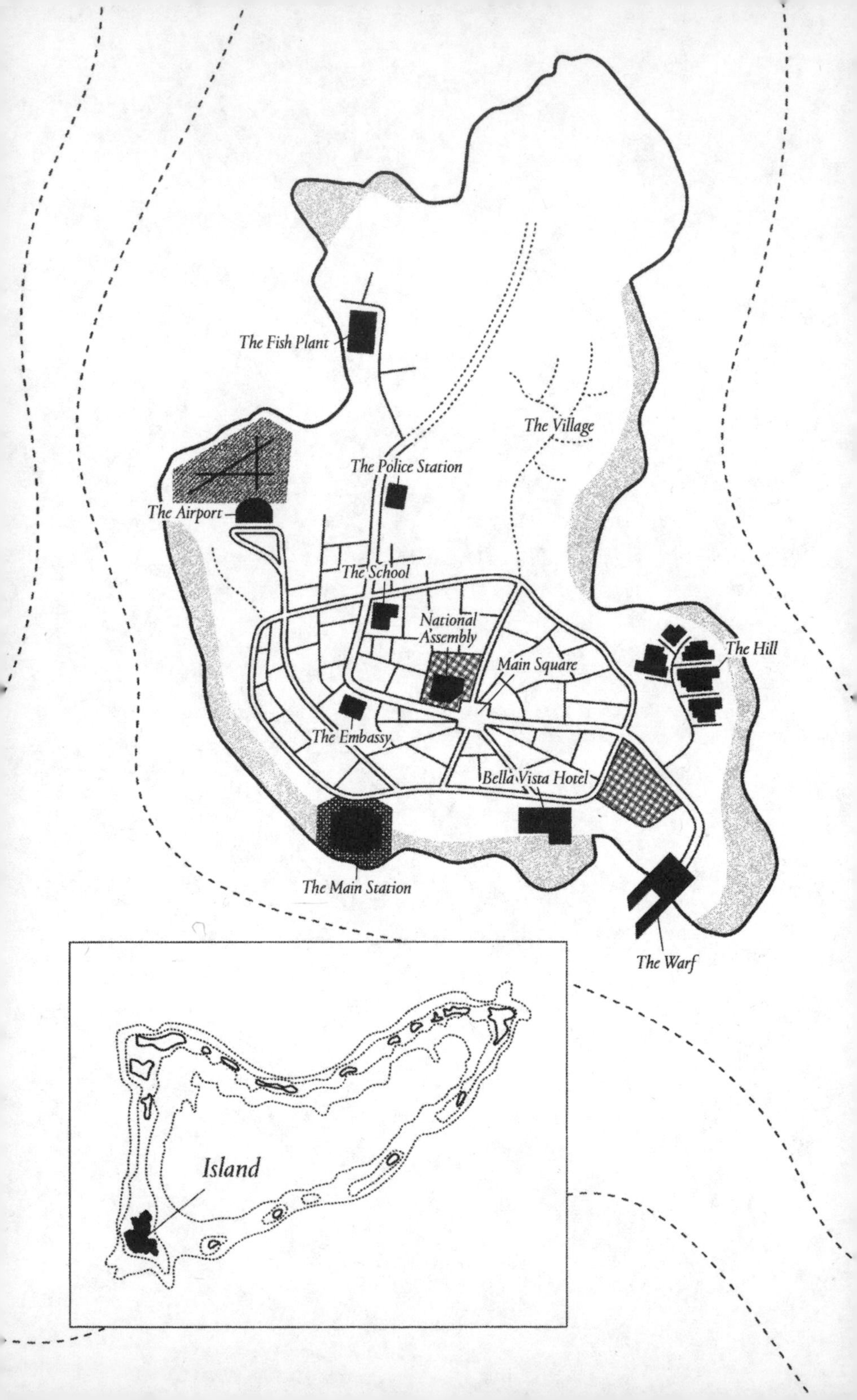
The Fish Plant
The Village
The Police Station
The Airport
The School
National Assembly
Main Square
The Hill
The Embassy
Bella Vista Hotel
The Main Station
The Warf
Island

ONE

It was not gradual. For at least several seconds Lota lingered, drifting among images from dreams she no longer recalled. Then the images vanished, the dream dissolved. She sat up in bed, already fully awake.

Her clothes had been laid out carefully the night before and now she dressed quickly in a pair of army-green cargo pants and a cobalt football jersey with the Brazilian national team's logo on the front nearly rubbed out.

The room was rented. Up three crooked flights of stairs in an old cable company building that used to house the foreign workers. These days, foreigners hardly ever came to the island and, whenever they did, they were flown in and out at the north end. They did their work at the new cable station that had been constructed there, and never actually set foot in town.

Lota had been in the room six months, but it was still nearly as bare as when she'd first arrived. She'd hardly unpacked, was still living out of a single suitcase. There really was nowhere *to* unpack, even if she'd wanted to. The room had no closet, or drawers of any kind—only a single bed in the corner and a small table beside it, which supported a cheap porcelain lamp. Also on the table were Lota's mobile phone and a glass of water, half drunk. Her suitcase, in the middle of the floor, gaped.

Opposite the bed and next to the door were a small sink and mirror. A bar of soap, a comb, and a toothbrush balanced on the rounded edge of the sink. Lota stood in front of the mirror, gazing at her reflection in the spotted glass. The room was so narrow that if the door beside her opened she would need to step aside.

But the door never opened, except when Lota herself entered and left the room. No one came to visit, or even knew where she lived. Her family in the village believed she lived with her auntie Toni, in the shopping district. No one had in fact spoken with Aunt Toni in many years and she didn't have a telephone. It was safe, therefore, to say, "I am living with Auntie." Nobody questioned her, but neither would they have known where to look for her if they'd needed to. Lota went back to the village frequently enough that the idea never crossed their minds. She saved just enough of her salary, and she brought it home every two weeks, along with tinned meat, potato chips, toilet paper, and other odds and ends from town.

She worked at the fish plant, fifty hours a week, and when she wasn't working she was either at the gym or at headquarters. By the time she got back to her room, she just fell into bed —sometimes without taking off her shoes.

Lota splashed cold water onto her face and examined her reflection. The mirror was chipped in the corner and the glass rusted. In places it was difficult to tell what spots were the spots on the glass and what spots were her own. She was naturally freckled, like her redheaded grandmother, but it wasn't white blood that ran in their family, her mother used to say. It was fire. The family could count back one thousand generations, knew how they were related to the sea, the sky, and to the hot lava that boiled beneath them. But like practically everyone else on the island, her mother never spoke of the family's white ancestors: the Irish and German settlers who'd come for the sugar trade, their colonial masters, or those—from all over Europe and America—who'd arrived on the island along with the first telegraph wire.

In the old days, "white ghosts" had flooded the island and practically every islander was employed by one. The grandparents recalled this time often now, but whenever they spoke of it it was always as if the "white ghosts" had just been passing through. As if they belonged—and could only belong—nowhere, to no one.

Yes, in those days, the old people said, there'd been a station, long since demolished, nicknamed "the old chateau." It had had something like fifty rooms, including a billiard room, a dance hall, and a library. There'd been little electric bells in every bathroom that when rung would almost instantly summon a Chinese servant.

After the war, a new station was constructed with none of these finer points. It was located underground in an old fallout shelter with twenty-four-inch-thick walls; the only luxury in the place was a wall of showers where employees could wash off radioactive material in case of a nuclear attack.

But at least there were still jobs. Lota's father had been employed there, briefly—and her grandfather and great-grandfather before him. But in less than a generation, everything had changed. Ø Com, the Danish outfit that acquired the station in the late seventies, laid off nearly all local workers, then simply stopped hiring.

They built an even newer station on the island's north end. What had once been the "new station" became the "old" or the "main" station and the even newer one was referred to as the "outer station"—if it was ever referred to at all.

Mostly, because no one who lived on the island had ever set foot there, they didn't call it anything, and half the time they even seemed to forget it existed. The work at both stations was done remotely these days, using computers, or else was too specialized for the undertrained local employees. Technicians and engineers were flown in for monthly service trips, and though a handful of islanders had been hired at the main station as janitors, desk clerks, or guards, no one but foreigners ever visited the outer station. It was as if, even before it was constructed, it had already disappeared: every official depiction of the island after 1982 left the entire northern end—occupied by the Empire, and by Ø—entirely blank.

The island's history was another blank spot. Except on very rare occasions, no one spoke of the day that, nearly fifty-five years ago, they'd looked up and—miracle of miracles!—seen snow raining down slowly from the sky. Or about the sixteen years they'd spent after that living as refugees on the Surigao coast.

They didn't talk about the war, either—in which more than half of the island's young men had fought and died on behalf of the Empire. Or, except in passing, of the telegraph days, or of sugarcane, or of sandalwood, or of coconut oil. It was really no wonder, then, when you thought about it, that, aside from stories of boiling hot lava and fire, no one seemed to recall exactly how light skin and red hair had got into the blood.

Lota's own hair was not red, but she had her grandmother's pale skin. As a child she'd been teased for it, sometimes mercilessly. But her mother had said, "You're stronger than they are," and Lota knew that she was right. She'd fought fiercely, thrown herself into each brawl like a dog, but each time she'd come home scratched and bruised her mother had just shaken her head: "That's not what I mean."

It was not until the seventh grade, while disinterestedly flipping through the pages of her history textbook, that it occurred to Lota that she was white. The book had fallen open to the first page of the chapter "Colonial Society and Economy," and underneath the chapter heading was a faded black-and-white photograph that depicted a European farmer on horseback surveying a group of workers in a sugarcane field. It must have been something about the way it was shot: the farmer in the foreground, his large face overexposed so that it appeared almost blank, and the workers in the background—more like shadows than human beings. For the first time, Lota realized that what separated the European from the workers in the field was not only that the European surveyed the scene from above, or that he wore a handlebar moustache and a grim expression on his nearly blanched-out face. It was the *difference* between his blanched-out face and their shadowed ones.

Her flesh began to crawl. For a long time, she'd been acutely aware of the colour of her skin but she hadn't, until that moment, connected it to the subject of "Colonial Society and Economy" or thought of it in terms of race. So that was all it was, she thought: there was a simple explanation. Her pale skin was no more mysterious than the pages of a history book.

She began to pore over them. She emptied the library, learning about the first waves of migrant workers to the islands, then about the colonial land grab, the foreign investments, the second wave of migrant workers, the faltering industries, the strikes of 1867 and 1872, the third wave of migrant workers, the strikes of 1898, the riot of 1912 . . .

She didn't care anymore when the other kids teased her, and as soon as that happened, the taunts abruptly stopped.

"What did I tell you?" her mother had laughed.

Lota felt neither proud nor ashamed now; she felt simply curious. What had once been fable and mystery, completely beyond her ability to know or comprehend, suddenly seemed navigable—a complicated but ultimately chartable course of bloodlines and records. But when she asked her mother where her own ancestors had come from, and with which wave, her mother only shook her head. "You're an islander, Lota."

"But we weren't always," Lota had insisted. "We had to have come from somewhere! In the first wave, there were workers from Australia and the Philippines . . ."

"Lota! You're an *is-lan-der*."

But Lota continued to read—secretly now. And because the taunting had stopped at almost the precise moment that she understood the historical cause for the colour of her skin, she forever afterward associated knowledge with power. A year later, when her mother was diagnosed with breast cancer, she checked out library books on the disease and its treatments, and lectured her mother on the latest medical advances, supplement regimens, and recommended healthy eating habits.

"Lota," her mother had chastised her, "just because you know something doesn't mean you can change it. God does not always, so simply, reveal his plan."

But by that point, Lota had read her way well into the twentieth century. She knew about the nuclear tests and the controversy surrounding both the resettlement and the return to the island. She was not only curious anymore.

"It's the island!" she'd burst out one night, her eyes smarting with the effort it took not to cry. "It's poisoned! Don't you get it? It's the *island* that's making you sick!"

They never should have come back, Lota informed her mother. The radiation levels were simply too high. Who knew what was even now—only semi-buried—seeping out of the earth.

"Pshaw!" her mother had spat. "You're reading too much, getting all these funny ideas in your head. Life is not always so easy, Lota, and it is not for you to judge. God makes choices for—and through—us, not the other way around. We have to accept both the good and the bad."

"Accept!" Lota wailed. "What does that even mean? 'Accept'? Don't you ever wonder why it's always us doing the accepting? Why nobody else ever does?"

"So that's it." The soft, yielding tone that always resonated in her mother's voice whenever she spoke of her faith, or of God, had given way to a harder, more exacting note. "So, Auntie G's right. You're too good for us here. Leave, then, why don't you? Go away. Become a doctor, a lawyer; live on the mainland. Come home once a year!"

Lota had looked at her mother—her bright eyes flashing at her like underwater lights—and felt deeply ashamed. It was true Auntie G had often told her she was smart enough to leave the island if she wanted to. She could come back with a diploma, Auntie G said, do big things, both here and abroad. When her auntie talked like that it didn't sound small and selfish the way her mother made it sound. For the first time, Lota realized just how impossibly thin every promise she might make—if she ever did leave the island—would seem to those left back home. She'd be celebrated, of course. Everyone who left the island was. Even her mother, despite what she said, would hang Lota's diploma on the wall and brag about the money that she made overseas.

But she would also be scorned.

"Maybe they'll give you a diploma right now," Lota's mother had said—without even looking at Lota. "You seem to know everything!"

Lota lowered her eyes, which had flooded with tears, and made a solemn promise to herself that, no matter what, she would never leave her mother *or* the island. But even as she said the words to herself, she knew—or hoped—that it was a promise it would at some point become necessary for her to break.

There was a noise in the hall. A rhythmic shuffle as someone climbed down three flights of stairs, then paused on the landing. Then there was the jangle of keys, the catch of a lock, the sound of a door swinging open. After a moment or two, the door closed again firmly with a click.

Yes, before she was even out of middle school, Lota had known: it was as impossible to leave the island as it was to remain. But then another option had presented itself. She'd met Kurtz, had joined Black Zero. And now, after three long years of training, they were ready. By midnight, the acting government of the island—President Vollman's absurd little puppet regime—would be overthrown and a brand new social and political order would be born.

Lota picked up the comb and began to tug at her hair.

They'd gone over every detail. Every possible thing. They'd visualized the progression of the day until they could have attempted the coup in their sleep—and did, almost nightly. So that even now, while everyone else on the island was waking up not knowing—while everyone else was waking up thinking it was just an ordinary day in which nothing would, or could ever, happen—for Lota and the rest of the Black Zero Army it was as if the events of the day had already occurred.

They'd storm the embassy first, then take the cable station. They'd alert the capital only once the station was secure. If the Empire deliberated in granting the Army their few demands (recognition of the island as an independent state; acknowledgement of its new leadership; imposition of a 24 percent tax rate on all Ø Com profits), they could, they would warn, simply shut down the cable system. The island was the main gateway of information traffic in the Central Pacific, and even a minor disruption of that flow would have a ripple effect costing billions in global revenue. All that was needed to completely dismantle the system was the login information—or a knife.

Lota exhaled slowly, pressing the breath past the point where it seemed to naturally stop.

Which was not to say, of course, that it was a *fait accompli*. Lota knew that she couldn't forget that. She knew that she had to feel—really *feel*—the way that, at every moment, absolutely *anything could happen*. That, Kurtz had told them, was the principle of total revolution. The possibleness of each moment had to tremble inside them. They had to feel that possibleness, had to act upon *that*.

She picked up the comb again and began to tackle the knots that had collected at the back of her hair.

Because possibleness could go any which way. Yes, there was always the chance, Lota reminded her reflection, that something unforeseen would interrupt, throw them completely off course . . .

The comb snagged. Lota tugged harder. She always got a little stuck on this point; preferred to close her eyes and see the future already arranged, in little patterns. When she was forced to admit the presence of the unanticipated, the unforeseen, she began to feel irritated in the same way she did whenever her mother or Auntie G mentioned God—or whenever her brother Marcus, who'd been recruited ten years ago to join the Empire's Pacific Command, mentioned freedom, patriotism, or the promotion system for enlisted navy men.

And yet, at the same time she knew there came a point when there was nothing more they could do in advance, nothing more they could prepare. She'd reminded them all of this fact just last week, when Verbal—recently promoted to chief of staff, though he was barely older than she was and had less balls—had argued that the date be pushed back again, this time to the beginning of July.

Kurtz was reasonable. She never cut in or shut anyone down. She'd just nodded when Verbal said this. "Verbal has suggested that we push our date back again." It was what she always did when anyone spoke in session—an aggravating habit, but one that, on other occasions, Lota understood.

This time, though, she was unable to restrain herself. "But . . . but that's ridiculous!" She'd turned first toward Verbal, then toward Kurtz. "What now? We can't possibly take *everything* into account."

She'd never spoken out like that in session before, and her own voice startled her. Usually it was only Norma or, on rare occasions, Mr. Joshua or Hal who interrupted Kurtz or challenged her in any way. But Lota had particular cause to be irritated that morning. Less than an hour before, Verbal had caught up with her on her way to the station.

"I—I think we could have something special," he'd told her. Between bites of a sandwich.

"What's that?"

". . . Special."

Lota pretended not to know what he was talking about. She'd known Verbal all her life. They'd played together as kids, swapped comic books, jumped off cement breakers down at the wharf. They'd even kissed clumsily once, several years ago now, after a hotly contested game of Bust, which Lota had won. Lota had lurched back, her face burning. She'd made some excuse or other—she couldn't remember what now—and ran all the way home.

Later, by way of apology, she'd told Verbal about the Army and suggested, in a roundabout way, that he join. Almost immediately, he did. Ever since, they'd been polite to each other, nothing more.

"We should talk," Verbal said, still chewing his sandwich.

"We are talking."

"No, I mean . . ." He stopped and grabbed Lota's wrist so that she was forced to stop, too. Her stomach leapt. Her palms sweated. The little salivary glands under her tongue began to leak.

Verbal took a step toward her and Lota stepped back. How, she wondered, *at a time like this . . .*

"There's nothing to talk about," she said quickly.

"Lota," Verbal said. "Lota, listen to me."

She'd been attempting to shake her wrist free, but now she paused—surprised. No one from the Army ever used her real name. She'd been Zilla, not Lota, for such a long time that hearing her old name gave her a physical jolt.

So maybe she was lying when she said there was nothing to talk about; she wasn't made out of stone. But it just didn't make sense, Verbal talking to her like this. Between bites of his sandwich. It didn't make sense, him deliberately reminding her of who she was, or had been—as if he actually wanted to get them stuck in the past.

Again, Lota tried to shake herself free.

"Listen," Verbal said. "Lota, listen. I love you."

Lota tried to wrench her wrist back. "No," she said, after an excruciating pause. "You don't."

Verbal let her wrist drop. Lota did not immediately retract it. She looked at her semi-open hand that now held, and was held by, nothing. She felt suddenly very sorry for herself, and for Verbal. For her own hand.

"It's just . . . it's just . . . not *now*." Her voice was thick and low and Verbal did not immediately understand. Then his eyes flickered. He grabbed her wrist again and, in an exuberant voice—as if the whole thing, whatever it was between them, had been settled—said, "Fine!"

When nothing had been settled—nothing at all.

Lota retracted her hand a second time. "What I mean . . ." She'd found her voice again. It established itself, a hard edge between them. "What I mean is, we shouldn't be thinking about this right now. It . . . it isn't the *point*."

Verbal was grinning at her.

Lota started walking—more quickly than necessary. "We'll be starting all over again," she said. "Everything will be different." She shook her head as she walked. "It's impossible to know what we'll want then. What we'll need . . ."

Verbal had caught up to her. He leaned in carefully—their bodies didn't touch. Lota could feel the pressure, the particular shape of the distance between them.

"Some things won't change," Verbal said. His tone was light, teasing even, but Lota didn't hear it. She whipped around.

"That's not true," she said fiercely.

Very briefly, the distance between them collapsed entirely. They collided. It was Verbal this time who took a step back. They stood looking at each other, both of them angry now, their faces just inches apart.

Verbal's eyes were set very close, Lota noticed. Like two deep pools. It was remarkable, she thought, how easy it would be just to—disappear.

"That's not true, *Verbal*," Lota said again. Her jaw was clenched now and her lips trembled. "*Everything* will change," she said, hardly trusting her voice. "You've got to understand that. All right? *Everything!*"

TWO

Rachel stared at her phone: no message. She'd called Ray just before she'd gone to bed, a little after midnight island time. She'd be up for another hour or more, she'd said, but he should call any time—shouldn't worry about waking her.

Rachel tapped the voicemail icon and for the tenth time in an hour saw that there were no new messages. She tapped the recents icon and saw—again—that there hadn't been any calls since the previous day, and no calls from Ray since the day before that. She'd caught him briefly on Wednesday, just before he headed out to drop Zoe at school. They'd spoken for less than two minutes. A blustery "Oh, hi, Rachel." (For some reason Ray always sounded surprised these days when he picked up the phone.) "Everything good? Sure, yes, everything fine here. In a bit of a rush, of course." (A laugh.)

Rachel had clenched and unclenched her jaw, had refused to be brushed off. "How's Zo?" she'd asked. Her voice loud, suddenly—falsely upbeat.

"Good, good," Ray had answered quickly. "She wants to talk to you, of course, but we're on our way out the door. *Zoe?* Yes, *now*. All right. Thanks, Rachel. We'll talk later. *Bye*." He'd hung up.

Rachel pushed her phone across the table. It did not slide far.

Had he actually *thanked* her? Rachel replayed the conversation in her mind, but even with the help of her willing imagination, she couldn't manage to end the exchange on a different note.

Now it was Friday. Thursday in the capital. She'd called three times, left two voice messages, and still there'd been no response. What on earth, she wondered—midday on a Thursday, when they hadn't spoken to each other properly in a week—was preventing Ray from calling back?

She shook her head and poured another few mouthfuls of cereal into the milk left at the bottom of her bowl, then ate them quickly. She was going to be late.

Well, who cared? She hated being late. Hated arriving flustered, out of breath, hated starting the day out apologizing. But this was her last day in the office. By this time next week she'd be back in the capital. Whatever subtle reproach she might feel this morning from Monique downstairs or from Bradley when she passed him on the way to her own office, next door—none of it would matter.

Her worries about Ray and Zoe would disappear, too. Yes, very soon now she'd be laughing at herself over how she'd let her imagination get the better of her; over how much meaning she'd given to the simplest things. She'd get off the plane and everything would come into focus. Ray would be there, waiting.

A fresh haircut probably, and his spring coat on (it would still be brisk in the capital, even in early May). And there Zoe would be, beside him. Looking a little older, of course—but still looking exactly like Zoe. She'd be grinning—showing off her missing front tooth, which she'd already proudly revealed over a video chat last Tuesday.

After all, it wasn't as though this hadn't happened before. Whenever Rachel and Ray had spent time apart, they'd always felt the distance. Ray would grow increasingly abrupt—to the point of being downright terse. Rachel, in reaction, would become more sensitive.

"It's like walking on eggshells with you," Ray would say. "You take everything *so seriously*."

It rankled Rachel more than it should when he said things like this. Of the two of them, it was Ray who was the worrier, the *serious* one. It frankly annoyed her, embarrassed her sometimes: how needlessly anxious Ray could become—even in the most relaxed of social gatherings, among friends. She could see it even when no one else could. His eyes would brighten. He'd raise his voice, tell jokes that were purposely bad—sometimes even be a little mean.

It was quite amazing, actually, Rachel had observed, how many people in the foreign service were not especially cut out to deal with other human beings. Increasingly, as she moved up the ranks, she'd noticed it. At least half of them were clearly diagnosable.

At least with Ray, though—at least at the beginning—there was a sense that where the "edges showed" there was also the possibility of *getting through*. She remembered the thrill of it the first few times he let his guard down with her: it was like stepping through a curtain. But it had been a long time since she'd felt like that with Ray. She needed physical proximity, she needed to touch him, to feel that ripple—something moving underneath.

She wiped her mouth and deposited her bowl in the sink. It was not gone, she told herself. Something like that didn't disappear. It only got hidden for a time, submerged beneath all the distracting details on the surface of a life. All of which—she was quite certain—would dissolve instantly the moment she and Ray actually saw each other again.

Rachel ran the water and watched the last of her cereal milk disappear in a single stream down the drain. No, they'd never really been able to do *abstract*, but because of it there was nothing sweeter than those first few hours in one another's company. It was like sinking into a warm bath. They'd barely speak; they wouldn't need to.

She glanced around. The place looked exactly as it had when she'd first stood in the doorway with Zoe and Ray, nearly two years ago now. She recalled her feelings in that moment: it was as if she'd just had the wind knocked out of her—and she'd been on the island for less than an hour.

Her mood had improved when the boxes arrived. She'd dedicated six straight hours to unpacking; then—feeling pleased—had poured both Ray and herself a drink and toasted to making "the most" of everything.

She was proud of her ability to make a home for herself and her family wherever they went. Also, she just loved unpacking.

When she was younger it had even embarrassed her: the undeniable pleasure she took in objects. In their physical weight, in the way they could both lend shape to and—at the same time—be shaped by a room. Someone like her, she figured—someone who basically lived out of a suitcase and hadn't had a paying job till she was nearly twenty-five—shouldn't care about *things*. But then, of course (as she was quite comfortable reasoning with herself now), they never really were just *things*. They were an archive, a record, a way of keeping in touch with the parts of her life that might otherwise have simply disappeared.

In any case, Rachel had taken pleasure in moving her possessions into the apartment at the beginning of her stay and now she was taking even greater pleasure in moving them out. She'd sent the bulk of everything ahead by post. Except for a few changes of clothes, the rest had been carefully tucked into her suitcase—which had now been lying open on the bedroom floor for several weeks.

She gazed contentedly at the clutter-free marble breakfast bar, at the glass coffee table that, for the first time in months, she could see through—clear to the lacquered parquet floor. Earlier that morning, she'd taken down the family photos and, because she hadn't yet put back the ultra-glossy hotel art they'd replaced, the walls, too, were pleasingly bare.

The framed photographs she'd stacked in a pile and slid into her carry-on bag. There was a picture of herself posing proudly in front of her first bicycle, one of her parents in the early days of their courtship, an awkward portrait of Ray and his extended family on the steps of his grandparents' colonial home. Then there was a series of Ray and Rachel from before Zoe was born. There they were: leaning their heads in and grinning into the camera in front of Angkor Wat, in front of the Sydney Opera House, the Eiffel Tower. After Zoe came along, the photographs were all of her. Zoomed in, so that she appeared to have no context.

Rachel's phone buzzed; her pulse quickened. But it was only her driver downstairs, indicating that she was already late.

Right. And besides (Rachel tried to assure herself, as she slid her phone and a set of keys into her purse and made her way to the hall), it was still only yesterday. For Ray, that is, as for everyone else back in the capital, it was only slightly past two on the previous afternoon. There was still time. He was probably waiting for the evening—hoping to find a quiet moment, a time when he wasn't either rushing between the office and the school, or the school and the office, or standing in the checkout line, or . . .

Rachel paused in front of the mirror by the door. She looked at herself with her lips slightly pursed, smoothed her hair, and applied a tiny bit of powder to her cheeks. It was a little secret she had, just between herself and the mirror: she was incredibly vain.

She glanced sideways, as though to catch her own reflection off guard. She appreciated the curve of her slim neck, the slant of a high cheekbone. It was just that she'd been such a late bloomer—had taken so long to feel comfortable in her own skin. Sadly, by the time she had, her beauty, such as it was, had already started to fade. But then maybe that was part of it. Maybe she only ever really started to feel at home in a place once she knew she wasn't going to get to stay there very long.

She pursed her lips again at the mirror and, satisfied, stepped out the door. The door shut and locked automatically behind her.

Though from the beginning of her stay there'd been talk at the embassy of a "proper" residence, the plan—like almost every other plan that had been spoken of over the course of the twenty-one months she'd spent on the island—had not moved even a provisional step closer toward realization. Everyone still spoke of it as though it were only a matter of time. The hotel suite was just a "temporary" measure—like just about everything else on the island.

Rachel's tenure, too, was only ever supposed to have been "temporary." After a one-year contract, she'd been asked to stay on. *Three more years.* Anyone can do anything, she remembered Ray saying shortly after she'd accepted the position, for *three years.* And besides, it wasn't as if (Ray pointed out) they had a choice. She'd been offered a tremendous promotion—to the position of first secretary—at *this* point in her career.

Still, Rachel had replied cautiously, it simply wasn't worth it if the risks began to outweigh the gains. She could still talk to headquarters, let them know that *under the circumstances* a three-year term on the island simply wasn't tenable—wasn't *safe.*

"The circumstances?" Ray had asked, his face purposely blank.

Rachel had felt her face get hot. She hated it when he did this—made her spell things out for him. But he always seemed to insist.

"It's one thing to *choose* not to recognize the risks for yourself," she'd said firmly, "but it's another thing not to recognize them for *Zoe*. Honestly, Ray, do you think all of this is going over her head? She gets called names *every single day*, Ray, and you know yourself"—she raised a finger at him—"you *must know* that it's just a matter of time before it's more than just names. Goddammit, Ray . . ." Her hands flew to her face. She stood there, massaging her temples, shaking her head at him, blinking back tears.

When she could trust her voice again, finally, she said, "I don't want to live like this, Ray. I don't want to just sit around like this, just . . . waiting."

These were the circumstances: Ray had the blackest skin anyone on the island had ever seen, Rachel some of the whitest. Zoe's was—similar to many of the islanders—somewhere in between, but because of it she'd been taunted near relentlessly ever since their arrival. Several times each week she came home from school reporting "bad words" that referred either to the colour of Ray's skin or to the fact that Rachel's had practically no colour at all. And still Ray had continued to insist that the problem had nothing to do with the colour of *anyone*'s skin.

"Well, how *could* it?" he'd said. "She looks exactly like the other little girls. And besides"—he'd paused, shrugged, purposely averted his eyes—"this isn't the first time Zo's been picked on and it won't be the last."

The cruelty was not so much in what he said but in how he said it. Offhandedly, as though the thing hardly needed to be discussed.

Rachel lunged—raised her fist at him as if to strike. He and she stared at one another—and then at her raised fist between them. "How dare you," Rachel said, before lowering her hand. She and Ray were roughly the same height. As she brought her hand down, she leaned her face in toward him, forcing him to look her in the eye. "*How dare you* say something like that."

The cruelty—as she was forced to reflect later—was that she knew it was true. Even as a baby, Zoe hadn't been like other kids. She'd avoided eye contact, been painfully shy. Now, at six, she talked to herself and, honestly, most of the time seemed to prefer her own company.

It was difficult for someone like Rachel—who'd always felt obligated to at least *appear* confident and self-assured—to understand. It was, perhaps, the one thing that still connected her to her own parents, who—for a brief, sweet, and now just barely recalled time in her early childhood—had actually had her fooled. She remembered, a little wistfully now, how she'd at one time believed them to be everything they imagined. She'd thought them fearless, intelligent, cultured; above all, *rich*.

Now, of course, she recognized them for what they were: solidly middle-class people from sensible penny-pinching Presbyterian stock—decent enough folk who'd worked hard to balance, on the one hand, their aspirations toward upward mobility with, on the other, an innate sense that they were fundamentally unworthy of what they already had.

But there'd been a decade or so before Rachel began to notice the signs of obvious strain—of the way that her parents struggled, together, but more often against one another, to appear better off, better educated, and more apparently in love. Once she noticed it she couldn't unnotice it. It began to cause in her a profound embarrassment that bordered on physical dread.

This was a feeling she still experienced—now not only on account of her parents. Because of it, Rachel respected her daughter—was even slightly awed by her at times. But this did nothing to change the fact that, deep down, she still held on to the fervent hope—no, the actual *belief*—that it was only a matter of time before Zoe "caught up" (that's how her mother always put it), became just like everyone else.

Ray knew it. He'd flinched slightly when Rachel leaned in toward him. But he hadn't backed down.

"You always need there to be some reason," he'd said. His voice was cold, but the meanness in it had ebbed. His eyes looked softer, rounder—like there was something at the bottom. Rachel had certainly got to him—but it wasn't a good feeling this time. "You really don't understand anything, do you?" Ray asked.

Rachel took a step back.

"It's like you're always looking for something, or"—Ray's voice sharpened in his throat. For a moment it felt dangerous—"or *someone*," he continued, "to blame."

"Fine," Rachel said. Hot tears had sprung into the corners of her eyes and she took another step back, turned away.

But then over her shoulder: "It really doesn't matter *what* it's about, though, does it?"

She wasn't prepared to admit that Ray was right, exactly. It was just that, when it came to certain subjects, she and he both knew that she was immediately out of her depth. Until recently —until Zoe was born—that had never really mattered. She'd felt proud of the difference that existed between herself and Ray—proud that she understood and could respect that difference. But when it came to Zoe. When it came to her own daughter . . . How *dare* Ray suggest that she didn't understand.

"No, it won't matter *what* it's about," Rachel said, "when it's not just name-calling anymore."

She hated herself a little for needing, as usual, to have the last word, but in this case she couldn't help it. Ray was acting purposely obtuse. He knew as well as she did how thoroughly violence permeated the island—and how much they had at stake.

Although it was true that, so far, their own lives had been well isolated from violence, to presume they were somehow *exempt* was just as wrongheaded as it was to play the victim; Rachel had been arguing as much for nearly two years. It was not something that could be hidden any longer, she'd insisted, not something that could be simply patched up. The rift that had grown between rich and poor on the island, as well as between inside and out, threatened—eventually—to swallow them all.

If you wanted statistics, hard facts, Rachel had plenty. Since the collapse of the fishery, at least 67 percent of islanders were unemployed. The money they received from government pensions was spent on alcohol—or supported the one industry, besides telecommunications, that had ever thrived on the island: the manufacture of cheaper and cheaper forms of methamphetamines. According to the latest global health poll, over half of the island was addicted to one form of the drug or another. This was a statistic Rachel had cited at countless meetings with the ambassador and representatives of foreign aid. She permitted herself a little pointed emotion when she added that the youngest addicts were no older than her own daughter: six.

After a moment or two of silence, Rachel would shift to a more practical note. The problem didn't originate on the island, she'd say, and it couldn't be contained there. There was simply no way forward either for the island *or* for the Empire without breaking down the imaginary borders that existed between them—and accepting responsibility for the mistakes of the past.

What she didn't say was that she only sent her daughter to the local public school because there weren't enough foreign kids on the island to merit a private elementary. Or that she had her daughter picked up and dropped off every day by a driver; or that since her arrival on the island, neither she nor her family had engaged with the local population in any way, outside an official capacity.

This last point had to do, of course, with "issues of security." The sorts of issues that were mentioned so often at the embassy that no one wondered anymore exactly what they were—or perceived the disconnect between the level of caution advised and the fact that, except for a handful of isolated incidents, foreigners on the island had never been the target of any real violence. They simply weren't "part of the equation."

Well, precisely! And yet, Rachel acknowledged, her own family's situation was more difficult. There came a point when you simply had to choose, she told Ray: big picture or small. Of course she hated the idea of "running away" just as much as Ray did—possibly even more. But they had their own family to think about now, and wasn't it a bit foolish—self-aggrandizing, even—to imagine that their *personal decision* about whether to stay on the island or go would make a difference to anyone?

She could see it all too clearly. Two more years of arguing for "clear policies" and "centralized strategic planning." To whom? For what? As she'd been told countless times now, "every imaginable step" had already been taken: an imported foreign police presence, educational outreach programs, support groups for battered women and abusive men . . . None of it, so far, had made the least bit of difference. People continued to talk about having their faces "rearranged" the way they talked about cricket, or the weather. Only the week before, a teenager had been nearly killed in broad daylight behind Josie's canteen over something less than ten dollars.

There was an important distinction to be made, Rachel informed Ray, between taking responsibility for one's life and safety and "running away."

Still, for some reason, Ray had resisted, and it was not until some weeks later that he finally admitted that something was wrong.

"Ray!" Rachel had shrieked when Zoe walked in the door after being dropped off by Grigor at the end of the drive. Zoe didn't speak; she didn't need to. She had her arms stretched out in front of her and Rachel could clearly see the places where her forearms and wrists had been chafed nearly raw.

"Ray!" Rachel had shrieked again—as though Ray had inflicted the harm on his daughter himself. Then she flew toward Zoe. "Who did this to you?"

Zoe began to sob.

"Tell me!" Rachel begged, her voice nearly pulsing with anger. "Tell me *who did this*!"

But Zoe was sobbing too hard to speak. Rachel reached for her again, but this time Zoe pulled back reflexively. As usual, Ray—standing there like a long shadow against the wall—looked to her like a safe retreat. Zoe ran to him, flung her thin arms around his waist.

Ray's arms closed around her. "Let's calm down," he said—both to her and to Rachel. "Let's all just calm down."

But it was a long time before either of them calmed down enough for Zoe to tell them what had happened. When at last she did, Rachel had exploded a second time—she couldn't help it—and the whole thing had started over again.

Three girls, Zoe told her parents, had pinned her to the fence after the last bell—in plain sight of the gate—and twisted her skin on both arms until it burned. "They said . . . bad words," Zoe sniffed. "They told me to say them too, but I wouldn't —I didn't."

"What bad words?"

Zoe sobbed loudly; Ray shot Rachel a reproving glare.

"What bad words?" Rachel asked again. She hovered above Zoe, her jaw set. She knew goddamn well what words they'd been—even if Ray wanted to pretend that she didn't.

But Zoe only pressed her face harder against Ray's shirt and spoke into the cloth. "I didn't say them!" she said. "I didn't say any bad words."

"It doesn't matter, honey," Ray said. "It wouldn't matter if you did."

Zoe's little body stiffened. "But I didn't," she insisted. "I *wouldn't*."

"Okay," Ray said, stroking his daughter's back and looking steadily at Rachel. "You're all right," he said—more to Rachel than to Zoe. "Everyone's all right now."

But they weren't all right, and both of them knew it. After Zoe was in bed that night Ray paced the living room angrily, and Rachel wept.

They'd call the school to complain, of course—and yet they worried that drawing attention to the problem would only make things worse. "We should keep things in perspective," Ray said at one point. He was standing with his hands dangling at his sides, blinking into the glare of the TV—turned to the ten o'clock news. He'd become heavier in the past year or so and, though Rachel knew it wasn't what required her attention at that moment, she noticed that there was something in his posture that accentuated the added weight. "We should remember," he was saying, "that we're talking about *chafed wrists*. It's the sort of thing that could happen *anywhere*. I mean, that level of aggression in kids, it's clearly impossible to avoid."

Yes, Rachel thought. He really shouldn't stand like that. It made him look a little . . . sad, ineffectual. Decidedly middle-aged.

What she said was: "This isn't about you or me anymore, Ray. It isn't about our careers. About how much *we* can take."

Rachel faxed an official complaint to the capital the next day. Was the situation "untenable"? Did she feel that a "direct threat" was posed in the country of residence to either herself or her family? After only a moment's hesitation, she'd checked "yes," and then again, "yes." Two weeks later they were making arrangements for Ray and Zoe to leave the island. Rachel, it had been agreed, after a somewhat disorienting meeting with the ambassador, would stay. The ambassador assured Rachel that he was, of course, *sensitive to the situation*; but with rotation schedules and personnel shortages, she would certainly be doing everyone a favour if, knowing that her family was out of danger, she'd consider staying on at least until early May.

She'd agreed. Without consulting Zoe—or Ray. Well, really (as she explained to both of them afterward), she was in no position to refuse. Everyone had been remarkably supportive, nothing but sympathetic from the start. The ambassador had even personally apologized—and, as though reading Rachel's mind, assured her that the decision wasn't at all likely to have a "negative impact" on either her or her husband's career.

"Times have changed," the ambassador had told her, smiling benevolently and giving his head a quick toss so that his neck cracked sharply. He straightened again, looking relieved. "Yes, you've come in at a good moment, Darling," he said. "Times have certainly changed." Some of the old guard would sniff, no doubt, he continued—would wonder what a "hardship tour" was these days, when one was permitted to choose one's woes—but it was clear that the old guard were being left further and further behind. "It's remarkable when you think about it," the ambassador went on, chuckling softly to himself. "Given the way that nothing ever seems to change at all . . ."

It was true that even over the course of Rachel's own brief career she'd seen clear signs that things were beginning to shift—and would continue to. It was impossible not to notice, for example, how, as you moved from the outer to the inner offices, the staff got whiter, maler. In less than a generation, these central offices would be inhabited by those (like Rachel) now located in the outer offices, and all that would be left of the old guard would be their nearly featureless images, which—for who knew how many years yet—would continue to stare down at them, disapprovingly, from the bank of photographs that lined the main hall.

No, requesting to leave a post on such reasonable grounds would not be held against either Rachel or Ray—Rachel felt confident of that. But she also saw no reason to push their luck. When she'd agreed to remain on the island until May it had "made sense" to everyone. Now, though, she got the distinct impression that both Ray and Zoe resented the situation.

She tried to tell herself it was only her imagination, that it was all in her head. Of course, *as a woman*, she was—one way or the other—going to wind up feeling like she was letting everyone down. *Of course* she was going to feel that the decision she'd made was stubborn and selfish rather than inevitable (the way she was quite certain they both would have felt had Ray been in her shoes).

Knowing this changed nothing, however, and—more and more—Rachel suspected that she'd misread things from the very beginning. That Ray's saying the decision "made sense" was just another way of saying she'd be heartless to choose it; that agreeing it was "the only choice" had included the silent amendment: "if, that is, one is more interested in one's career than in one's child."

Well, why hadn't he come out and said it then! Did she actually need to remind Ray that the decision had been as hard on her as it had been on Zoe and him? That she'd chosen to remain on the island not out of selfish desire (she'd give just about anything to be putting in easy time back on the mainland, like Ray; to never have even set foot on the island!) but based on a series of practical calculations that would soon benefit them all? After this, at any rate, it would be simply impossible to say they hadn't "put in their time." Ray knew this as well as Rachel did. And also this: that if it hadn't been this island, it would have been another. And in the scheme of things, even Rachel had to admit . . . it hadn't been so bad. A scrape. A few bruises. But they would come out stronger for it—she was nearly sure of it. The time she'd spent apart from Ray and Zoe—something just less than six months—would pretty soon disappear entirely, would hardly be recalled.

The telephone buzzed in her purse. She slid it out and stared expectantly at its lit-up screen. But it was only Phil Mercer, CIO of the major telecommunications company—Ø Com—that managed a base on the island. Calling to ask for another favour, no doubt. *Jesus Christ*, it was her last day in the office.

Reluctantly, Rachel tapped the screen. "Phil," she said.

"Hate to bother you, Rachel."

"No bother. I'm just on my way out the door. Why don't I—"

"No, listen," Phil said. "I wanted to catch you while you weren't in the office."

Rachel could see Grigor out the window, leaning against the hood of his car, staring into his phone. "You know it's my last day, Phil," she said. She'd paused on the second-floor landing and now she leaned her weight against the narrow banister. "What's up?"

"You've got to talk to Vollman."

Ed Vollman had been acting president of the island for going on fifteen years. The island didn't have any stipulation on the length of time any president could serve, and there was no reason to suspect, at this rate, that he would not be the president for another fifteen. Every election the same islanders trickled into the polls and, so far, there'd never been any genuine opposition. But then there had never been anything to oppose. Vollman was president in name only. The island was an independent nation, but everyone knew that all the real decisions were made by the capital—and by Mercer, by Ø.

So what was this about talking to Vollman, when she'd never talked to Vollman and no one else had ever talked to Vollman? Except about vacation rentals and imported booze.

"What's Vollman got to do with anything?"

"Everything," Phil said. He sounded breathless. As though he were walking uphill. "He's got us blocked. Some old paperwork—hard to explain it all over the phone. I'm telling you, though, it's a real mess. Something about a clause in the original cable deal—somehow no one caught it till now. Vollman dug it up. Can you believe it? Vollman!"

Rachel's phone buzzed again. Her heart leapt. But it was Grigor, wondering what was keeping her.

"Look, Phil, I've got to go."

"The cable station," Phil continued, his voice going uphill. "The old paperwork says it has to be physically located on the island. I mean, we're talking about a deal that was drawn up nearly two hundred years ago, Rachel. For *telegraph wires*. And Vollman, for some reason, isn't budging. He says it's a matter of national pride. I kid you not, he pulled that on me. *National pride*, he said. And I said—"

"It's not like you to get so upset," Rachel interrupted. "I mean, really, Phil. To you—to Ø—when has no ever meant no?"

By this point, nearly all of Ø's South Pacific cable lines had been transferred to sea stations; the island was the company's last land access point. Practically speaking, this meant that—compared to competing cable networks—Ø had almost zero regulations.

"The future has been decolonized," Phil had told Rachel proudly when they first met. They'd been walking on the pier, behind the old station—which offered one of the best sunset views on the island. Phil had stopped walking and was looking out over the water. The sea, Rachel remembered, had been almost eerily calm, reflecting in diminished colours the vibrant red glow of the setting sun. He'd extended his arm toward the water—spread his thick fingers as if to indicate the way that everything, if it had not yet already dematerialized, was just about to. "We've never been wireless," he said. "And as far as I can tell, we're never going to be. But at least we can clear out a little of the old mess, give ourselves a little breathing room. The wires aren't the problem—it's what they're tangled up with. All the other companies, you know, they just keep laying one technology over the next. Fibre optic over coaxial over telegraph. Even if there's a better route, a more direct one, it doesn't matter to them. The old route is always safest, and safest—to all the *other* companies—means best. Every time a new layer of wire is laid, history repeats itself. We're wireless in the same way we were once diplomatic, or imperial. All the old hierarchies, all the old imbalances get laid along the exact same lines. But for *us*, there is no history. For us, there's only the future. And the future," Phil had concluded, winking at Rachel, "*has* no allegiances."

Now he was saying, "It's not that easy this time. This is a major obstacle, Rachel. A *major* obstacle. I want you to talk to Vollman."

"Okay, sure. And tell him . . . what?"

"Tell him he's got his fist jammed down the wrong hole! That if he wants a future for this island, he's got to let go of the past. There's no *money* in it, tell him! The past was all about land and loyalty—how much real estate you owned and how you got it and why. But the future is liquid, tell him. It's about money, and nobody cares where you got it. I've told him all this myself, of course, but maybe, coming from you . . . He likes you, Rachel. He does. He's going to miss you." A pause. "We all are."

Grigor was beeping again. Rachel slung her purse over her shoulder and continued down the stairs. "Thanks, Phil, thanks," she said dryly. "But I really don't see what I could—"

"You know, us old guys, we all look and sound alike. But *you* . . ."

"Oh, I see."

"Yeah, it's like that. No offence intended, all right? It's an advantage."

"I'll talk to him."

Rachel hung up the phone.

THREE

Lota took another brief, hard look at herself in the glass, then stepped toward the door. She hesitated. Feeling certain she'd forgotten something, she glanced back—looked searchingly around the little room. She saw her bed, unmade; her suitcase, left open—though it hardly contained anything; the sink where the tap, which had been turned off firmly, continued to drip, contributing to a permanent stain.

There was nothing that could be left behind.

So why had Verbal wanted to stall everything? Why had he wanted to find some way to keep them forever only *approaching*, rather than actually realizing, their goal? Lota found her mind returning to the question unwittingly. He was like every other island boy that way, she thought—didn't want anything to change, *really*; was afraid that *he'd* be the one required to change it . . .

But then, it hadn't mattered in the end—Verbal's suggestion. When Lota had thrown up her hands and said, "We can't possibly take *everything* into account," everyone else had agreed.

First Norma—peeking out from beneath her pulled-down cap, then Hannibal, Baby Jane, Mad Max, Bruno, Alex DeLarge . . . Pretty soon even Verbal—with only a fleeting glance toward Lota—had nodded and, along with the rest of them, raised his fist in the air.

"*Fidel Castro*," Kurtz had said in a low voice when they were quiet again, "*Fidel Castro* himself once said that, for revolutionaries, there are never any obvious truths." She lifted an eyebrow and a single hand in the air. "There may," she continued, "also not ever be any obvious times. The horizon is always shifting, after all." (Briefly, she seemed to look directly at Lota.) "What's up ahead remains ahead, out of reach—permanently unknown. Castro, he said—" (she raised her voice slightly, but the hand came down) "that *obvious* truths were an invention of imperialism, that they are used by those who are big in order to oppress those who are small. *Well*," she said (and raised both hands this time), "let us not—any longer—be oppressed by the obvious!" (She lifted her eyes to the ceiling. Lota, along with the rest of the soldiers—Verbal included—lifted theirs, too. Lota's heart soared.) "Let us instead embrace the uncertain!" Kurtz shouted at the acoustic-tile ceiling. "Let us advance fearlessly into the unknown!"

It was a few minutes past eight; as Lota left the building the sun had just begun to peek its way over the tallest trees. Bo Brown, reeling home drunk, spotted her from across the street and waved. He'd been singing the refrain of a popular radio song she just barely recognized, and now he raised his voice so that she clearly heard the repeated last lines of the song: *nothing brings me down . . . no, no, no.*

Lota waved back.

No, nothing. Nothing brings me down, Bo sang.

A few early-morning regulars were sipping tea outside of Josie's canteen and did not look up when she passed. She walked quickly. Past the broken clock tower, the hospital, the grocery store—everything still closed, even the hospital, deserted looking. A tree next to the grocery store shaded a few kids sneaking in an early game of two-up before they were called in to get ready for school. Past a few new kit homes, a row of rundown tract housing, the school, then a few more new homes. Finally, she arrived at the depot. The police dog, Juno, a big red mastiff pit bull cross with watery eyes and a torn ear, got up reluctantly, barked once, then settled back down. A mix of sullen disinterest and affronted longing—typical for the breed. The dog stared at Lota as she crossed the yard and disappeared around back.

She knocked once; a moment or two passed before Kurtz opened the door.

All the fans were on inside, and the wall-unit AC was blasting musty cold air. Everyone was standing around, drinking coffee and Kool-Aid. In the middle of the table, a half-eaten box of doughnuts gaped.

Lota pulled up a chair and reached for a jelly doughnut. The doughnuts had sweated in the heat and were sticky. Kurtz checked the clock on the wall, then sat down at the head of the table. Everyone else grabbed a chair and sat down, too. It was as if she'd fired a gun at the starting line; they all nearly jumped.

Kurtz, though—as usual—took her time. She always began every meeting the same way, by staring around the table, careful to look each one of them in the eye. After that, she invited them to report on whatever they'd learned or observed since their last meeting. They all had to come up with something.

"Mrs. Wah is dealing again." "The embassy closed early this week." "Mr. Gregory's wife left him." "I no longer feel afraid."

Kurtz would write everything down, and when they had gone around full circle and everyone had said something, she'd nod her head, and the crease that ran like a crooked scar between her eyebrows would—very slightly—deepen.

But this morning, after carefully catching each one of their eyes, she simply said, "That's all of us—except Pinky and Khan. They'll meet us at the embassy." Then, drawing herself up and narrowing her eyes so they seemed almost to become one, she said: "This is it, friends. This is history. A moment that will now repeat itself forever—that can never be taken back."

No one spoke. The AC hummed; the clock ticked like a bomb on the wall.

"Is everyone ready?"

Still no one spoke.

"All right," Kurtz said. "Let's go."

Nobody used their real names. A security precaution—but an island superstition, too. It was inconsiderate and unwise to speak the names of the dead because they were still too much like the living; they got distracted and jealous, lonesome, confused. It was entirely possible that if those who'd only recently passed heard their name spoken, they'd get turned around and come back, disrupting the balance between this world and the next.

By giving themselves new names, Kurtz and the rest of the members of her Army indicated that they now had only one direction to go—and had made the commitment all the way.

For a while it had felt odd to Lota—like a game—but after a while she got used to it. When she did, she found it was a relief to come into the station, to leave "Lota" behind. At the station she was always Zilla—and she held herself differently. As Zilla, she doubted herself less, was calmer, cooler, more self-assured.

It had been a joke at first, choosing the names of villains from popular movies or comic books or television shows. "Ha! I'll be Alien." "Hello, Leatherface!" "What should I be?" "Ha ha! Baby Jane?" But it had been a long time since the names were funny—or referred to anything beyond themselves. They were just names now: Mystique. Hannibal Lecter. Killmonger. Jack. Joker, Predator, Dr. Szell . . . But they were names with power.

"A villain is only a villain to those who fear her," Kurtz had said. "A villain is only a villain to those who tell her she doesn't belong." So far, Kurtz had explained, in the whole of human history, we'd only ever managed to replace certain elements in the system and even "total" revolution had failed to completely change anything.

"We have to learn to think differently," she said. "We have to think like our ancestors did. Before they were taught to be afraid of the darkness. When they still understood that the world and everything in it is based on a complex relationship —*not* a clear separation—between what we call good and evil, darkness and light."

And another time: "You're never going to be a superhero. Anyone here, by the way, because they want to be a superhero?" She stared at them, a mocking smile playing at her lips.

No one said anything. Or moved. Or even seemed to breathe, until Kurtz relieved them all with a short laugh. "Let me tell you," she said, "you're in the wrong place for that! Have you ever seen a superhero that *looked* like you?" Again she laughed sharply. "That *talked* like you?" Her voice hardened still more. "That came from an island that, so far as the people who make the movies are concerned, doesn't even *exist*?"

Their name, Black Zero, had been taken from the DC comic books. Black Zero was a villain in some stories. In others, it was a terrorist organization, or a computer virus. In all cases, Kurtz told them, it was dark, sinister, and defied rationale. When it was a human being, it had no fingerprints and its most destructive weapon was "the secret in its brain."

"We also have a secret," Kurtz had said, standing in the middle of the police department's basement room, chin lifted, feet spread wide, thumbs resting on the top of her belt. "Look deep inside yourself," she'd said. "Past all the superhero garbage, past the hope—which you've always known is in vain—that things are going to work out for you the way they always seem to work out for them. Past the impossible, deluded fantasy that you're going to wake up one day and find yourself—a hero—right at the centre of the story.

"Our secret is, it's *not our story*. Our secret is, it never has been. Our secret is that we exist, and have always existed, outside of every system through which they've tried—repeatedly—to either save or destroy us. The plots of their stories are always the same, right? More or less? What's different—what changes, what can never be defined—is what shapes the plot from the outside. It's why every movie has a sequel, right? Why they can never arrive at the end. Because what threatens them—what they try to seize or destroy—is bigger than they are and can't be reduced to a simple arc." She drew the top of a triangle in the air. "Or a 'happy' ending, either—an ending that brings us, more or less, back to the place we began. Because what threatens them is whatever it is they're *not,* and that's bigger and more powerful than they are—and can't be eliminated.

"That's the secret." Kurtz was practically whispering now, but everyone heard. "*Our* secret. Look down," she said. "Deep down. Find the part of yourself that knows that. The part of yourself that *knows* that history does not have to endlessly repeat itself. That *knows* we can do things differently this time. Find the part of you that feels silenced, excluded, overlooked, betrayed . . .

"Think back!" she commanded. "Think back to the stories that your grandmother told you. Think of the way her voice shook whenever she spoke about leaving the island—or of coming back again. And if she never did speak? *Think of that silence.* Think of all the empty places in the world where her voice—her story—is not."

Kurtz raised her hands from her belt and extended them toward her assembled soldiers, who—hearts slamming in their chests—stared back, horrified, invigorated, and amazed. "That," Kurtz said, gesturing with her arms in the air as though the blank, silent, unknowable thing she was referring to were a physical object that existed between them. "That silence is our secret. And because of that secret," she concluded, "we can't lose. I promise you. With that secret, we'll win every time."

Lota had first heard about Kurtz from her younger brother, Miles. That had been over three years ago now, when he was still working at the police depot. Less than a year later, he got fired for stealing confiscated drugs. "It's not like everyone else isn't doing it too," he'd told them—which, of course, had only made things worse. Afterward, he admitted it would have been better if he'd just told them he was sorry.

"Yes, sorry! So, so sorry," he would say later, in fun, when it was too late to be sorry. "I won't do it again, Officer," he'd say, "*promise, I won't . . .*"

He was always nearly out of his mind; his nose running, his eyes all wobbly. Even while he had the job at the station he was like that—which is why the job hadn't lasted too long.

"They meet in the basement," Miles had told her. "I see them go in. One after another—every fifteen minutes or so. So they think nobody notices. Roy has a hand in the business, I guess. Must figure there's no place safer than right under everyone's nose."

Roy was Mad Max's real name. He was second-in-command to Kurtz and also to Frank Ramon, the chief of police. Frank was almost eighty and had lost most of his wits, but he was kept on out of—equal parts, probably—inertia and respect. He'd been around forever; could still remember the bombs. Could still remember the island before the bombs. Before they'd all been shipped off, and then back again, and there was nothing for miles but cement and sand.

Remember! You bet he could. He was like all the old people that way. They didn't talk about it much, but they couldn't forget.

"What kind of business?" Lota asked.

"Oh, Sister." Miles grinned. "Some real bad-ass revolutionary shit—swear." He opened his mouth to laugh and Lota could see that his gums were bad. "And that woman," Miles said, still laughing. "She went away, you know, lived on the mainland for years. Thinks she's Che Guevara or some shit, that she's gonna change things. Change the island—right?" He gave another short shout of a laugh, choked on it a little, then spat.

Lota had noticed the woman walking past the school on her way to the station on plenty of occasions. She was tall, all angles, with a long forehead and tight, close-cropped curls turning grey at the edges. A deep line ran like a scar between her surprisingly close-set eyes.

Lota didn't need to be told that this woman had lived off island. She held herself differently than island folks did—looked less like an "auntie" and more like someone out of the pages of a book: a doctor, a poet, an Egyptian queen. It was, in any case, not at all difficult to imagine that at least some of the rumours were true. That she spoke six languages, had gone to university and to prison; that she was an artist, a political radical, a gun runner, a spy . . .

But until Miles told her about Kurtz and Mad Max and the basement of the police depot, the idea that the island could change had never once crossed her mind. She'd only continued to feel the terrible impossibility of living there. Increasingly, she'd felt it—as she entered high school; as her mother got sick, and then well, and then sick again. No way to escape, she'd thought; then—angrily—no way to remain.

After Miles told her what he had, Lota began to watch for the woman every day. She stood out back of the school gymnasium after class let out, straining in the direction of the depot, and feverishly rehearsing what she would say: "I know." (She'd mouthed the words to herself.) "I can help."

Only a few days passed before she saw the woman. Long neck arched, eyes fixed straight ahead, sailing toward the horizon like the figurehead of a tall ship. Lota's heart leapt, her mouth felt dry. How could she possibly approach this person? What—she suddenly wondered, even after all the time she'd spent thinking about it, and rehearsing her lines—could she *say*?

She almost let the moment pass. Almost let Kurtz sail on, out of sight. But then some other part of her took over and she gave a kind of a yell, then double-stepped to catch up.

"I—I wanted to speak to you," she said, hating the way her voice sounded. Like one of the kids on the wharf begging for a dime.

She forced herself to continue. "I've heard of you. Of . . . what you do, and I wondered"—she paused, swallowed, then finished weakly: ". . . if I could help?"

The woman had stopped in her tracks but she'd kept her eyes level, pointed straight ahead. Now she turned slightly.

"So . . ." she said. Coolly. As though without interest, or concern. "You've heard of us? You know what we do?"

Lota blinked, nodded. "Yes," she said—suddenly uncertain. "Something."

The woman was not really looking at Lota anymore, but Lota felt her eyes burning into her anyway. She'd never felt more exposed.

"You're very young," the woman said. "Only—what? Sixteen?"

Lota shook her head but didn't correct her. (She was seventeen—eighteen, come fall.)

"You've got your whole life ahead of you." The woman had begun walking again; Lota followed. "You could get married next year. Fat. A couple of babies by spring. Or, what? I get it.

You're too smart for that. So win a scholarship. Study literature in England, why don't you? Go see London, go see Paris, France."

It seemed that the woman had quickened her pace; in any case, Lota was having difficulty keeping up. Again she double-stepped and they walked nearly to the clock tower in silence before the woman stopped. She turned and looked directly at Lota for the first time, and so fiercely that for a moment Lota thought she might strike.

"Are you prepared to give that up?" The woman's teeth were bared and clenched. She practically hissed out the words. "Are you prepared to give up *everything* for something that might not even happen? For something you might not even see?"

Lota's heart beat quickly, and her mind raced as she tried desperately to understand what was being asked.

"Think about it," the woman said. "Think about it three weeks, and if—after three weeks—the answer is yes, *then* you come find me."

Three weeks passed. Then three months. Then three years. Lota got up slowly and pushed her chair back into position under the table. She touched her hip, feeling automatically for her weapon. Then she turned toward the exit, following the direction of Kurtz's gaze. In another moment, Bruno would push the depot door open wide, she would walk out of the building, and everything would change.

FOUR

How, Rachel wondered as she made her way down the stairs to the lobby, could Phil seriously expect her to tell Vollman to let go of the past? It was all the islanders had ever had. Until recently, they hadn't even had an island: a nuclear test had rendered it completely uninhabitable back in 1965. The local population had immediately been evacuated. The plants had withered, the buildings had crumbled, the beaches had been blanketed in a thick layer of radioactive dust and ash. In all likelihood, no one would have ever heard of the island again except that, in the mid-1970s, its dispossessed people began campaigning to move back home. Protests and demonstrations had briefly garnered international attention. Even Rachel's father, who'd never been, as he put it, "political" exactly, remembered.

Had he been in support of the island? Rachel once asked. Well, of course! Who would *not* be in support of a people who, having lost everything, asked for literally nothing in return?

Images of the ruined island had been circulated widely, accompanied by portraits of islanders looking by turns lost, angry, defeated, and confused. They'd lived as refugees in the Philippines for a generation, were adrift there—haunted by nightmares, by demons. There'd been a rash of suicides; alcoholism had become endemic; domestic violence accounted for more than half of all local hospital records. Without a homeland, the islanders said, there could be no way of imagining the future. Without a homeland, they were disconnected from time itself—stuck somewhere between the present and the past.

No one who became involved in the matter at the level of diplomacy—as many soon did; the whole thing quickly became a public relations nightmare—had felt that it was in anyone's best interest to point out that, as far as anyone knew, the island (which had never really been an island at all, but an atoll, in the very last stages of its geologic existence) had no native inhabitants, that the dispossessed population had never properly belonged anywhere, or that the island was now so heavily contaminated with radioactive waste that any natural matter that still existed above sea level would need to be sealed under a protective layer of concrete and wire before anyone set foot on it again.

But where did that leave them? Even the islanders must sense it now, Rachel thought, that whatever energy had drawn them back—whatever they'd hoped to redeem or be redeemed by—had all but disappeared. A deep apathy had settled in. You could almost feel it—the way it clung, like the damp air. Rachel remembered getting off the plane for the first time, a sinking feeling in her gut. Disgust mixed with a sort of visceral dread.

No, she wouldn't be at all sorry to leave the island behind. It had started to get to her, to get under her skin. Time moved strangely. It was as if there was no way backward, or forward. No future, "liquid" or otherwise, no past—and so no possible way of letting go. Once, the old people on the island said, time had been balanced and whole, but now the demons had begun to slowly chip away at it; time itself, and everything suspended within it, had begun to fracture. There was less and less to grab hold of, more cracks to slip into, more ways to disappear . . .

Rachel pushed through the hotel door and her own image reflected back at her strangely. The horrible thought occurred to her that in the months she'd spent alone on the island, time really had been standing still. Or else progressing backward. That by the time she returned to the mainland it might already be too late: her career over, Ray having long ago forgotten her, Zoe grown.

The morning sun greeted her with its indifferent glare; Rachel winced. It was a ridiculous idea. She pushed it away and gave Grigor a quick wave. The island had certainly been getting to her.

And yet, she thought, as she made her way to the car, it was impolitic to mention what everyone, including the islanders, must have already secretly acknowledged to themselves: the main problem was that the island existed at all. She was sorry to admit it even to herself, but it was simply true. The island never should have been rebuilt; the project never should have got off the ground. Because, when it came down to it, all anyone was doing was waiting for it to disappear again. A clause in the relocation agreement, drawn up in 1981, stipulated that if and when—according to natural causes or an unforeseeable act of

God—the island should once again be covered by waves, territorial rights would immediately revert to the Empire. It was only, therefore, a matter of time. Even those islanders ignorant of the clause had to know that at some level. The island, and their existence on it, had only ever been provisional. Their return to it—like their exile—a temporary measure that served not their own interests but those of people and forces beyond them.

There'd been a lot of talk about accountability, of course, in the early eighties, but like most things it was all a matter of perspective. Rachel's profession had taught her that much. It was all a matter of how you looked at the thing, and from what angle, and how far you were willing to peer either forward or back.

She reached the rear passenger side door, which Grigor had left open for her.

After all, she considered, as she slid inside the car, it was one thing to identify—as her father's generation had done—who and what was responsible for the islanders having been displaced. It was quite another thing to identify those responsible for their having arrived on the island at all—or to know who was responsible *now*.

Except for a handful of colonial overseers, almost no one had come to the island willingly. They'd arrived in waves, following one industry or another—all of which had eventually pulled up stakes, leaving their imported workforces behind.

The only legitimate industry that had ever flourished on the island was the cable industry. The island was located exactly halfway between Los Angeles and Tokyo, making it an obvious choice for a stopping point along the first trans-Pacific section of the All Red Line in 1907—as well as for the first coaxial cable system, implemented in 1963. After the island was evacuated two years later, cable companies were forced to redirect their lines, using older and more circuitous routes. But the station, which had been built like a bomb shelter, remained intact, and the lines had already been laid. At the first rumblings of a possible return to the island, Ø purchased the station for a song and—before the islanders had even moved into their government-built homes—the most strategic Pacific cable hub had been instantly reborn.

But nothing else had been. Countless voices, numbers, data, stocks, bonds, news items, petitions, memos, advertisements, and petty observations whispered through the cable lines beneath the island all day long, but the island itself remained nothing but a hollowed bone. How, Rachel wondered again, could Vollman, or any of the islanders, "let go of the past" when there was nothing else to grab hold of? The nearest land mass was over one hundred kilometres away . . .

"Sorry. I got hung up," she said to Grigor. "Telephone call."

"Ahh!" Grigor grinned at her. "Raay! How is he?"

Now that she'd arrived, Grigor didn't appear to be in any particular hurry. He was sucking on a cigarette and leaning out the car's front window (a compromise; he knew it was not permitted to smoke in the car). His shirt was already sticking to him in the early-May heat.

"Good, good," Rachel said.

"And the little one? Isn't missing me too much?"

"It's difficult, of course . . ."

"Of course." Grigor dropped his cigarette and turned the key in the ignition. The car lurched forward; Rachel's stomach dropped. The ground seemed to shift beneath her and she had an uncanny sensation that she would never see either Ray, or Zoe, again. That she was moving steadily away from, rather than toward, them.

But why should she feel that way? She could count the distance between herself and her family in hours now, not months or weeks, or even days.

Her recent conversation with Phil returned to her—unbidden. "No offence intended," Phil had said. "It's an advantage."

An *advantage*. The word stuck like a fishbone. Rachel tried to pry it out—to identify its sharp end. The comment had been ignorant, of course, but that was nothing new, coming from Phil. What bothered Rachel was something else. Something she couldn't exactly put her finger on. She repeated the phrase a third and then a fourth time before it hit her. When the words ran through her mind, almost automatically now, it was *Ray's* voice she heard speaking them. *That* was the thing that stuck, that Rachel found difficult to swallow: ever since they'd arrived on the island, Ray had considered her to be at an "advantage." He'd begun to resent her for it. She'd felt it—undeniably. Without ever exactly putting it in those terms. It had begun slowly, at first—apologetically. But somewhere along the way, the resentment had become real, and (if Rachel was completely honest with herself) she couldn't exactly blame him.

Grigor made a sharp left and Rachel slid into the door, her shoulder banging heavily against the glass. Grigor glanced up and grinned at her in the mirror.

"Sorry!"

Rachel managed a hard smile.

But was it really too much to ask, she was thinking, for Ray to have been genuinely happy for her—*proud*, even? Just as she'd been—for the most part—every time he'd received recognition instead of, or ahead of, her? Why, she wondered, was it a woman's lot to be made to feel like this, even in her own marriage—with the one person to whom she'd ever felt close? Ashamed of her own success?

Grigor made another sharp left; Rachel braced herself. They pulled up sharply in front of the island's single set of traffic lights.

Of course, she wasn't being fair—she knew that. It had, after all, been Ray who'd insisted that she take the job. "You'd be crazy not to," he'd said simply, with a shrug. "I honestly don't even know why we're talking about it."

She tried to calm herself by keeping her eyes fixed, straight ahead, on the light. She dared herself not to look away until it changed from red to green, but almost instantly her eyes stung. She fought hard not to blink or look away. It was remarkable, she thought, how hard it was to concentrate on a single thing for something less than a minute and a half—to actually register the difference between one thing and the next.

But she wasn't making it up, either—she was fairly certain of that. There was an accusation in there, somewhere. In the shrug; in the way that, as Ray spoke, he hadn't exactly been able to look her in the eye: "I honestly don't even know why we're talking about it."

So maybe it was unfair! She'd certainly never said it wasn't. They were equally qualified—that went without saying. Their careers had followed almost exactly the same course. Ray had worked harder, no doubt. He was always so anxious to please, that was why. Success mattered to him more, on account of his upbringing. He was a black kid, adopted at birth by white Southern Baptists. Practically speaking, as Rachel liked to say, he'd been raised by wolves.

She realized that it hurt him when she said this; knew that, despite everything, he could never bring himself to fault his parents. They were good people, after all (even Rachel had to grudgingly admit that). Uneducated and short-sighted, perhaps, and as confused as anyone when it came to separating self-sacrifice from private desire, but good people, nevertheless.

Because of it—as Ray mentioned often, in their defence—he'd never, growing up, been made to feel anything less than worthy.

But that was precisely it—what Rachel had always found so disturbing. Ray had been "different" growing up, sure, but he'd also been "chosen." To be cut off from the past was, he'd learned early on, the only possible beginning, the only way he might one day be "saved." It had been a chance in a million, his parents had told him, but the chance was his, and he had every right to take it.

Of course, an ability to readily perceive what was so preposterous—and potentially dangerous—about the kind of assumptions Ray's parents had always made (assumptions which, to a certain extent, had become Ray's own) did not bring Rachel any closer to an actual understanding of Ray's experience in the world, she knew this. But until now, the implicit distance—or difference—that existed between them had never really seemed to get in the way. It had instead (or so Rachel had always thought) offered them a way of looking at each other and themselves—at the world, even—in a way that didn't just *presume* that difference could be swallowed up, absorbed within a single point of view.

And besides. As she was fond of informing Zoe whenever they failed to see eye to eye: like it or not, "understanding" was not the only perspective on a situation a person was entitled to have.

The light had changed to green without Rachel's noticing. They'd already lurched forward, were dodging motorbikes and stray dogs on the main avenue, only a few blocks from the embassy.

She would call Vollman the moment she got in—get that out of the way. "Us old guys," Phil had said, "we all look and sound alike, but *you* . . ."

Really, she should be offended—and *would* be, except that Phil never offended anyone. He was just like that. The perfect businessman. The type that, even when he said outrageous things, everyone, including Rachel, would just shrug or laugh.

She could play out the whole conversation in her head, knowing pretty much exactly how it would go.

"Darling!" Vollman would say (because everyone related to her professional career had always called her by her last name). "How are *youuuuuuu*?" (Vollman knew that, in the eyes of both the people and the foreign governments, his strength lay in his impeccable manners, his laid-back island charm.) "Oh, that thing with Mercer," he would drawl. "Don't worry about it. Don't worry about it!" And, after saying her piece, Rachel would put down the phone and take Vollman at his word.

She would *not worry about it*. That's right. Not even one little bit. After saying her piece, Rachel would put down the phone, gather odds and ends from her desk, make a few final telephone calls, do the rounds in the corridor, and finish the day off with a quick visit to the ambassador's office, where they'd spend a few minutes congratulating each other for the way things had—more or less—"worked out for everyone."

Yes. Things had worked out—they really had. She hoped Ray could appreciate that—if not immediately, then soon. She hoped he'd see how her remaining on the island really *had* made sense, that he could appreciate that the connections she'd made, even during her brief tenure on the island, would, very shortly, move them both well ahead. What made the island so inhospitable on a human level was, after all, what made it so significant on a global one. It had even been proposed by no less a figure than the Empire's chief security officer that the entire world would one day be controlled from the island precisely because it was exactly what it appeared to be: a near-people-less state that did not even have a natural land mass. Like money, government was becoming—had *no choice* but to become—increasingly invisible. Very soon, the officer opined, it would disperse itself completely—like data over the internet or "a fart in the wind."

Rachel remembered feeling increasingly uncomfortable as the officer spoke. It was like watching one's own place in the universe being methodically edited out. According to the ambassador, however, things had never been more exciting. "Just when you thought you'd been taken to a remote little outpost in the Western Pacific to wither away and die," he'd said to Rachel the first time she'd met him and Phil Mercer together, "you're actually right smack dab in the centre of the action." They'd talked fibre optics, global communication. A lot of it, frankly, had gone over Rachel's head. She'd felt only slightly better when, after Mercer had left, the ambassador admitted that he wasn't too clear on the details either, felt generally uneasy about a global telecommunications monopoly, and that much "remained to be seen." In any event, he assured her, there was nothing to worry about: they'd benefit either way. "If Ø goes all the way, we go all the way," the ambassador had said. "And if it doesn't—we still get a hell of a lot further than we are now." He leaned back, smoothed the lapels of his linen suit, and motioned for the cheque. He was a large man, impressive in his way. Kept himself fit, was naturally tanned, seemed not to sweat even in the late-September sun.

He turned back to Rachel. "Yep," he said. "This is the last major land-based information hub. Before anyone makes a penny in Hong Kong or Sydney or Rome, it goes through us. You never would have suspected it, would you?" Rachel had nodded, stirring her drink. She was puzzled by the plural pronoun but didn't ask the ambassador to explain. As far as she knew, Ø was a private corporation that had nothing to do with the Empire beyond a few subsidies.

The ambassador must have meant only that the money passed through the island itself, she reflected, its physical coordinates . . .

Her ice cubes were melting fast, from the inside out. The ambassador raised his glass. After only a moment's hesitation, Rachel raised hers, too.

It was important to remain as neutral as possible, she reminded herself—especially when it came to subjects she didn't fully understand. This was the whole point of diplomacy. If the ambassador had forgotten it, perhaps her own behaviour would serve to remind him. Yes, she thought. Despite, or because of, what one *didn't* understand, it was important to assert, and as much as possible adhere to, certain previously-agreed-upon codes.

She swallowed her drink and sat back—tried to relax. She made an offhand comment about the weather and decided, in advance, that she would not refuse a second drink if asked. It was hard not to suspect that it was all a bit far-fetched—an attempt, perhaps, on the part of the ambassador and Phil Mercer (who, though certainly companionable, was altogether unimpressive;

pot-bellied with bad teeth) at positioning within the sphere of influence a corner of the world best known as the planet's largest floating garbage patch.

They were sitting on the roof patio of the Bella Vista Hotel and Rachel could see, from that perspective, not only the entire town centre—a network of low concrete buildings, rutted streets, and leaning telephone wires—but the point at which the centre gave way to the periphery. To her left, she could see the rusted iron gates of the main station and, beyond that, the blank, uneven landscape. To her right: the wharf, the breakers, the endless sea. She understood the island's strategic importance, of course, but "the centre of the action," indeed! It was certainly possible, she concluded, to lose one's perspective.

Grigor made a U-turn around the treed median in front of Josie's canteen. They were only a minute or so away from the embassy now. "Well, say hello to the mister," Grigor said. "And to the little miss, too." Then he looked up so that his and Rachel's eyes met briefly in the rear-view mirror, and he winked. "Nothing else matters, right?"

The sun splashed through the window, filtering through the leaves of the lead trees. Rachel felt her neck and shoulders relax. She hadn't even been aware that she'd been leaning forward—braced against Grigor's driving, against Ray, against her own memories, against whatever was coming next.

What was she afraid of?

She leaned back, watched the light flicker and dance on the leather upholstery. "That's right," she said to Grigor in the mirror.

She felt happy. For the first time in weeks, months—in who knew how long. In fact, she felt positively elated. She'd been anticipating this moment for what felt like forever, but until now it had hardly felt real.

She was going home! To Ray. To Zoe. "Nothing else mattered." It was impossible to put a finer spin on it. Rachel could have kissed Grigor for reminding her.

"Grigor. Pull over, would you?"

"What?"

In the rear-view, Rachel could see Grigor's eyebrows raised, but he swerved toward the curb and hit the brake. An old man sipping tea in front of Josie's canteen looked up.

Grigor swung around in his seat. "Mrs. Rachel?"

But Rachel waved away his bewildered concern. She let herself out of the car and stepped onto the curb. The heat pressed against her; it was like another body beside her own. She made her way around to the back of the canteen, where the owner kept a motley array of souvenirs on a rickety table. Rachel had glanced at them once or twice before—careful not to let her eyes linger. She'd wondered where they'd come from, and if anyone had ever purchased anything. Except for a handful of nuclear-history buffs, the island was almost completely untouristed. It was not known for anything except getting literally blown off the map and, because it could claim no original peoples, had never had any authentic traditions of its own.

This fact became even clearer to Rachel as she sorted through the collection of mismatched objects on the display table. There were key chains shaped like the island, mushroom-cloud magnets, inexplicably a few Rastafarian badges, and an assortment of beaded hemp necklaces. She felt a little sheepish as she combed through the sad little display. She'd hoped, briefly, that there might be something that could be taken away. But there was nothing. No symbol, no simple souvenir.

She was just about to go when something caught her eye. A snake, curled in the shape of—yes, she was not mistaken—the Rutherford-Bohr model of the hydrogen atom. The symbol had been stamped or carved onto a circle of rough wood and strung onto a braided chain. Rachel picked it up and turned it between her fingers.

"Excuse me . . ." she said, generally. It was not immediately clear which, if any, of the old men lined up outside the canteen she should be asking. "Excuse me . . . How much for the necklace?" A long moment passed before there was any reply. She may have been the souvenir shop's very first customer, but no one seemed too eager to make a sale.

"Twenty," one of the old men said finally, without looking at her.

"I'll give you ten."

"Twenty," the man repeated.

Rachel shrugged and put the necklace down. But she knew that even if the man didn't relax on the price she would buy it. It appeared to her like her own time on the island—both treacherous and absurd. The perfect souvenir from a place whose history was a complicated knot of competing and often conflicting traditions: a place where the Dreamtime stories of Australian Aborigines, Confucianism, Islam, and Darwin's *Origin of Species* wove seamlessly into Catholicism and an adapted theory of nuclear fission . . .

"Fifteen?" Rachel asked hopefully. She'd never been much good at bargaining but felt she at least had to try.

There was no answer. Grigor had got out of the car but had kept it idling. Rachel was already late—and now she'd be even later. She picked up the necklace again and turned it over in her hands. She knew that the creation story told on the island was similar to the Aboriginal Dreamtime story that described another world, or dimension, where the sun and the moon, all the islands and stars, and every animal, plant, insect, and stone, had come into being. This Dreamtime included everything good and bad and made no distinctions between giving and taking away. It was a time outside of time, where every living thing on earth had already been born and died, where nations had already fashioned and destroyed each other, where every story had already been told.

How, Rachel wondered, had everything unravelled from there? Become fragmented and distinct? She wasn't certain if the dream stories ever properly explained that. According to one account she'd read, the ancestral spirits had begun to struggle with one another in a sort of spiritual survival of the fittest. But then another account depicted the Dreamtime's demise as a slow, degenerative process, more along the lines of radioactive decay.

What was certain was that the world had been cast adrift; that difference had been introduced; that the past had been separated from the present, the present from the future, and so on; that conflicts had erupted; that fire was born, and floods; that bombs were invented, and wars, and gambling, and drug addiction . . . What was certain was that the process was irreversible and ongoing—and would eventually result in the complete annihilation of the human race.

She fished her wallet from her purse. "All right, twenty," she said. She extended a bill in the direction of the man who'd named the price. The old man made no move to accept it, however, and Rachel hesitated for a moment—the bill flapping between her fingers a little in the very slight breeze—before taking a few steps forward and pressing it into his hand.

Grigor opened the door for her and Rachel slid into the back seat.

"Well, I didn't manage to get much of a deal," she said, but in fact she felt pleased. She examined the necklace again—traced the loop of the serpent's neck as it curved into the atomic spiral. Birth and Death. Creation and Destruction. It was all hopelessly entangled in the stories that were told on the island. It made her think of Ray, too—of his upbringing. Because just as in the tradition in which he'd been raised, the impending destruction of the world came with a promise: an original wholeness would eventually be restored. In some versions, the restoration of this original time really did resemble resurrection, but in others it looked more like the singularity: a total breakdown of general relativity, wherein all matter began to flow toward a single point, finally disappearing beyond the event horizon and eradicating space and time.

Grigor revved the motor and jolted his way down the main avenue, braking sharply at every stop sign without ever really coming to a stop. A few minutes later and they'd pulled up in front of the embassy's gates. It was a modest enough building, even for the island. A three-storey concrete structure painted rust pink. A small lawn was kept clipped and tended by the single caretaker, the ancient ex-cableman Coco Fen. It was one of only a handful of tended gardens on the island, and it made the building appear optimistic in a way that no one who had worked longer than a week or two inside the building actually was. Despite the presence of Ø Com and the ambassador's attempts to see things differently, there was no other way to spin it: the island existed beyond every imaginable sphere of influence—and every hope.

Rachel grabbed her purse, handed Grigor a significant tip, and shut the door behind her.

It made her sad, of course. Ray, too. "It would be one thing," she'd said sometimes, at the beginning, "if there was something *we could do*. But—there's not, is there?"

It surprised her to discover just how surprising the idea was. There being *nothing they could do* jarred sharply, she realized, with her understanding of the world as a logical series of steps that one could progress along, potentially endlessly. With her sense that, given the proper combination of positive thinking and sheer determination, nothing was ever entirely out of reach.

She knew that things didn't really work like that, of course, and had—ever since meeting Ray, perhaps—a certain appreciation for the way things *just happened*, were beyond anyone's control. But appreciating this did not make her any better a diplomat. Or any better a person. She still cringed—out of pity or fear, she didn't know—every time the young men whooped at her or she passed one of the old-timers on the street.

And yet somehow, especially in these last months, ever since she'd been alone on the island, the place had begun to feel almost familiar. Her father had been a local politician, a notorious ladies' man, and something of a drunk. Her mother, predictably, a repressed and brittle woman. She'd done everything she could to disguise this, of course, but still Rachel caught glimpses of her mother in the faces of the battered island women: the same vacant stare, as if the body's last defence was to leave itself more or less uninhabited.

And her father—Rachel caught glimpses of him, too. In the studied nonchalance of the older men. In all that stunted ambition, false bravado, angry desire . . . It was only ever just the briefest wave of recognition, then it would be gone. But the feeling unsettled, even embarrassed her. Because, of course, in point of fact, her past—not to mention her future—had nothing to do with the island. And even for a moment to imagine that it did . . . Well it was disrespectful, at best—both of the islanders, and what they'd suffered, and of her own privilege. But somehow, the more she tried to push the resemblances from her mind, the more they occurred to her. She would grit her teeth, think almost angrily of Zoe and Ray—of everything that she was moving toward, and everything she was leaving behind.

She did so now. Yes, she instructed herself as she made her way down the short walk to the embassy, she needed to concentrate on closing the distance rather than widening it again. Because, whatever the island people said, there was really only one direction for time to move in, and that was steadily forward. Every day, every hour now, brought her closer to home, to her husband, her child. Even now, for example (she pushed open the embassy doors, slipped into the empty hall), she was getting closer. Yes, this time tomorrow morning, Rachel thought, mounting the stairs, I'll be in an air-conditioned cubicle, high in the sky—well out of all of this.

FIVE

Lota was sitting in the van behind Bruno, the engine on. They were about a block from the embassy—could just make out the entrance. Could just make out Kurtz, approaching the embassy along the narrow walk. She appeared to be in no particular hurry, as if she had all the time in the world.

Well, what did she have to worry about? Christine was on duty that morning—one of their own. She'd landed the job a couple years back; a cinch.

In less than two minutes—Lota watched the clock on the dash—Alien would follow. With Christine's help, he and Kurtz would disable the guards. Three minutes after that, Lota herself, along with Bruno, Verbal, Hannibal, Joker, Alex DeLarge, Norma, and Baby Jane, would stream in through the unguarded embassy doors. Lota would follow Verbal up the main stairs to the minister's office, then to the first secretary's. They would restrain the foreign officers, using force when necessary, but at all costs refraining from violence.

Kurtz had been firm on this point. "This civilization is such," she'd proclaimed at the beginning of one of their final sessions, "that one has only to be patient and it will be self-destroyed." Her eyes had been fixed on the ceiling, as though waiting for something, or someone, to descend. But then she shifted her gaze so that she seemed to be staring directly at Lota. "Who said that?"

Lota didn't know.

Kurtz held her gaze. "Something diseased," she continued, "something poisonous has been 'eating into the vitals' of the nation." Her eyes drifted. "Congresses and parliaments are still 'emblems of slavery.'" They settled, purposely, on Verbal this time. "Who said that?"

Verbal blinked.

"Mahatma Gandhi," Kurtz declared. "The leader of the Indian independence movement that ended eighty-nine years of official British rule. Gandhi said, If you will sufficiently think over how poisonous and self-defeating the cultures and policies of the dominant civilization have become—you will cease to blame them for it. They rather deserve our sympathy, he said."

"*Sympathy!*" Norma spat. She was seated in front of Lota, perched in an excessively upright position at the edge of her chair. Her oversized clothing disguised her thin frame, and her newsboy cap was, as usual, pulled down low over her eyes. The only part of her body that was clearly visible was her hair, which she wore in two thick braids down the middle of her back.

Norma was only a few years older than Lota, and Lota remembered her well from elementary school and junior high.

She'd always been small, as well as smart, stubborn, and pretty in a way that made Lota feel shy.

Later, Norma hung out with some of the mainland kids. She became sarcastic, was notoriously impudent with both students and teachers, and managed somehow—just months before graduating—to get herself kicked out of school. It was rumoured that she'd spent a few years on the mainland after that, living with a much older friend of hers. In any case, Lota never saw her again until she showed up one day out of the blue in the basement of the police depot. She'd become aggressively thin in the interim—and introverted in a way that seemed belligerent rather than natural or essential now.

"*Sympathy!*" Norma spat again, in a voice that exploded from somewhere at the back of her throat.

"Yes," Kurtz said coolly. "Yes, sympathy—*above all.*"

Norma exhaled loudly in order to register her complaint.

"Because if we allow ourselves to be angry," Kurtz continued, as if she hadn't heard, "if we imagine we might somehow avenge ourselves against the mistakes of the past, we'll remain there. The future will be closed to us—a *fait accompli.*"

Norma's voice cracked out like a bullet. "But violence," she said. "Violence is inevitable, is a *cleansing force*. You've said so yourself. And how many times has it been used against us? You ask us to *sympathize*?"

Kurtz seemed to lengthen before them. "You haven't been listening," she said. She was staring hard in Norma's direction, but then her eyes lifted; she looked at each of them in turn. "Our *power*," she said, "does not consist in the mere repetition of actions or phrases. What we need is not to simply *give back* what's been given to us but to effect *an actual reversal*. To be ironic in the true, rather than the more common, sense of the word. We can't, you see"—she stepped forward—"simply employ the same terms, only this time in an unexpected way. We need to actually *undo* them—to defuse them from the inside, to make them ignorant again! We *need*," Kurtz said—she took another step—"to wrest irony from fate. We need not to *know*, any longer, where we're headed. We *need*"—she took a third step, was standing almost directly above Norma now—"to refuse their histories, their *violences*." She had her arms raised slightly, for balance or effect. "We need to refuse their expectations," she continued, "no, their *knowledge* of the way things will end!"

Her arms dropped. She stood looking at them—for the first time, Lota thought, as if she truly didn't know what would, or should, happen next.

Norma was silent. No one else risked even a sideways glance.

"Of course," Kurtz said, "when it comes to the station, it will be a different story." There, Kurtz explained, if they held their fire, they'd be annihilated in less than a minute. "So you can relax," she told Norma. "You'll have your chance to use a gun."

But then she lowered her voice again and narrowed her eyes so that they almost seemed to cross.

At the embassy, she warned, they were under no condition to shoot. "Not unless the *entire operation* is threatened, do you hear?" She paused. "And of course by 'entire operation' I do not mean *you*. *You*," Kurtz continued (but her voice was softer now, perhaps even a little bit sad), "are just a tiny drop of water, do you understand? A grain of sand. A single—already extinguished—star. Is that" (there was another weighty pause) "perfectly clear?"

"*Yes*," Lota had chanted—her voice responding before her mind had even properly made sense of what had been said. Around her, from every side: "Yes. Yes. Yes."

So, it didn't matter that they didn't understand. The word itself was enough. It filled the gaps, propelled them forward . . .

Later, Lota would puzzle Kurtz's meaning out at the fish plant, or in the few moments she was granted alone at night before being pulled—almost against her will—into a heavy, dreamless sleep.

Most of the time, she did end up feeling that she had come to some sort of understanding in the end. But sometimes she didn't. Try as she might, for example, she never could understand how any whole could be made up of parts that, on their own, more or less virtually did not exist at all.

It didn't matter. She got too caught up in the details. Verbal was always telling her so.

"*Yes*," something in Lota responded again now, just as Kurtz reached the embassy door. "*Yes*." As the door opened. As, out of the corner of her eye, she saw Alien begin his approach.

It was happening.

Yes.

Here. Now. Lota's heart thudded powerfully.

Yes.

And she—no matter how invisibly—was a part of it. She shut her eyes, practised the visualization exercise Kurtz had taught them. They had to not just be able to see it happening, Kurtz said. They had to *feel* it—somewhere deep inside them, in the blood, at the level of the DNA: the Army's *unconditional and absolute* victory over the acting government of the island.

Over and over again, they'd practised, together. Each of them with their eyes shut tight around the boardroom table, Kurtz at the helm. Her hair erect—framing her head like a halo. Her calm, steady voice leading them slowly, step by step, through the events of the day.

The exercise would always conclude the same way. "We," Kurtz would declare, "the people of this island" (here she would take a brief, sharp breath, pulling the air around them taut like a bow), "answer to no authority but our *own*."

There would be nothing but silence then, until, inevitably, the world began to return, very slowly. In the form of the buzz of the air conditioning, or the whine of a chair under someone's shifting weight.

Lota always fought it. She tried desperately to remain with the voice, with the events as they'd been, and continued to be, imagined, but she always found herself drifting. She'd feel an itch at the back of her throat, or else an image of her mother would flash, or the voices of one of her brothers would echo suddenly in her mind. Or else she'd start to picture herself explaining all about it afterward, about how everything had happened, her own part in it all. Or it would be Verbal. She'd feel his eyes on her with the sixth sense for that sort of thing she'd developed lately. It was as if they were connected by an invisible cord. Whenever he nodded, or shifted in his seat, she could almost feel it snap.

Alien now; it was nearly time. Lota watched him. Strolling along the outer path, dressed in a collared T-shirt, slacks. His weapon was concealed; his posture—like Kurtz's—unworried, nonchalant.

It was just so *different*, though, Lota thought—watching it happen in real life. There was too much detail, even for her. Now, for example, as Alien approached the embassy's door, she noticed the little cracks on the concrete, heard the hum of the sprinkler on the lawn, felt her own pulse in her throat and neck. She felt so overwhelmed by these excess details, which she'd so thoroughly failed to anticipate, that she could no longer recall—let alone visualize—what was supposed to come next. The future, she realized with a quick flutter of panic, was utterly, terribly blank.

She shook her head to clear it. She needed to focus—that was all. What did the cracks in the concrete or her own pulse have to do with anything?

Once the door shut behind Alien . . .

Three minutes. Okay. The images came flooding back to her; she shouldn't let herself get so distracted; shouldn't allow herself to begin to doubt. Three minutes now.

She looked around quickly. Bruno in the front seat; Baby Jane behind. Hannibal, then Verbal directly to her left. No one in the van looked as casual or as nonchalant as Kurtz or Alien had.

Maybe it was just a matter of proximity. In the van, they were all practically sitting on top of one another: she could see the perspiration standing on Bruno's forehead, hear Baby Jane's breath quickening, feel the way the blood was beginning to constrict inside Verbal's veins.

It had become almost unbearably hot, and it was as if all the air in the van was being slowly pressed out from the inside. No one looked at anyone else. All eyes were on the clock on the dash.

Two minutes.

Lota wiped her hands on her jeans. She hoped they wouldn't feel too slippery on her gun. She took a deep breath and tried to locate that place inside her where the thing was already done. She felt distracted, though, by the heat, then by the sound of the sprinklers, which continued to hiss outside on the lawn.

She glanced across the street. Watched a few kids, playing hooky, pass a single cigarette between them in front of a vacant building with the initials JPF scrawled in brilliant blue letters on the side.

Then, as though there'd been no progression at all: "Let's move."

The van door clicked and slid open. The hot air hit Lota like a wall. A moment before it had been too warm inside the van; only now did she realize how comparatively cool it had been.

Hannibal, closest to the door, leapt out. He was wearing khakis and a military beret his great-uncle had worn fighting for the Empire in the Second World War. His feet hit the gravel and he took off at a trot. Behind him, Joker. Then Norma, then

Verbal. Now it was Lota's turn. She could hear Baby Jane and Alex DeLarge begin scrambling out behind.

No one looked back. They trained their gaze on the back of the person directly in front of them and made sure they maintained a distance of approximately five yards.

Lota stared at Verbal's back. Sweat had darkened his shirt in a V-shaped stain. She was careful to keep pace, so that the distance between herself and the stain neither lengthened nor shortened.

Then Hannibal gave a shout and the pace quickened. She was through the embassy gate (five steps), had moved along the path (fifteen), up the wide concrete stairs (four more)—

But now she lost track.

Verbal was still in front of her. All right. She could still see the stain. But she could no longer calculate the distance between them—and then she no longer had any bearings at all. There was just a sudden rush of motion, a blur of colours, of bodies and sound as she moved toward—then through—the open doors. A surge of blood to her brain—then a feeling of intense relief. It was as if her skull had opened and every thought she'd had leading up to that moment, every doubt and misgiving, every selfish apprehension had been suddenly released. The cool air of the lobby blew through her emptied brain. Her veins opened like corridors, delivering oxygen to parts of her body that had never received oxygen before.

She made her way as if by instinct across the lobby toward the stairs. She didn't *need* any bearings now but her own. She climbed. Taking the stairs two at a time. She turned left

—automatically—on the third-floor landing. No, she needed no direction now . . . How many countless hours had she spent, after all, studying floor plans, visualizing their approach? She knew the place like the inside of her own brain. She'd practically created it—dreamed it up. The spinning fans overhead. The double glass windows at the top of the stairs. It was all hers—yes. And because of it, she could *feel* rather than see her destination at the end of the hall. She moved toward it instinctually—like a plant toward the sun, or a tree root toward water.

But she hadn't managed much more than four or five paces before her movement was checked. She doubled over—thought, at first, that she'd been hit by a physical blow. It was only after she'd raised herself again that she realized it hadn't been a blow but a sound: a gun had been fired.

Then two more shots rang out. This time Lota understood what they were and kept her balance. At the end of the hall the door to the minister's office was ajar. Just a moment ago, she'd been heading straight for it without even really seeing it there, but now she saw it plain as day. The rigid rectangular frame, the slant of light on the floor, and Verbal—feet spread, the top of his shirt still dampened by a V-shaped stain—standing squarely in the entrance, blocking the way.

Verbal.

Relative distances re-established themselves. Her arms shot out—a reflexive gesture. Almost immediately, she retracted them.

A darker stain had begun to spread its way across his shirt in the opposite direction. As Lota watched, the two stains—one spreading from above and the other seeping up from below

—began to take on the shape of an hourglass. Lota swallowed hard. She could not make sense of the way that the two V's ran together, the darker stain on the bottom spreading more rapidly now.

She swallowed again and looked past the stain, toward the minister, slumped at his desk. If it were not for the blood, which was beginning, with a steady rhythm, to drip from the table onto the floor, Lota might have assumed that he was simply absorbed in a difficult task.

But there was blood—and Lota recognized it. When she looked back at Verbal, she saw that the stain spreading on the bottom half of his shirt was also blood. She continued to stare. First at the hourglass and then at the minister and then back again at the hourglass. She felt the direction she needed to move in somewhere deep in her body, but something else—some immense pressure—held her.

The first secretary's office was just next door. Lota blinked hard, twice, in an attempt to make the hourglass and everything that went with it disappear. Then—by tremendous effort—she turned and plunged the few steps down the hall.

At first, the room didn't appear to be occupied. Lota looked around, but there was nothing to fix upon. Her vision wobbled. She turned—was just about to go. But then a sound startled her; a shrill, almost inhuman cry. Her vision sharpened. A tall, thin woman holding a phone to her ear came suddenly into view. She was wedged like a stick of furniture between the desk and a filing cabinet and didn't appear to be speaking to anyone.

Slowly, very slowly, Lota raised her gun.

The woman's chest heaved. There was another high, strangled sound. Lota's hand on her gun was surprisingly steady. She pointed it at the top button of the woman's blouse. It was not a steady target.

"*Shut up!* Put the phone *down*!"

The two women stared at one another.

Finally, the telephone clattered to the floor.

"Hands *up*." Lota's voice felt closer this time—more under her control. The woman must have sensed it, too. Almost immediately, her hands shot up.

Lota grabbed at one of them—keeping her right hand steady on her gun. Then she lowered her gun hand and unclipped a set of handcuffs from her belt. It was all much clumsier than she would have liked but at last she managed to secure the woman's wrists to the desk's upper drawer. The woman was forced to crouch awkwardly. She stared up at Lota from that position. Her mouth moved; it's possible she spoke.

A wave of nausea hit Lota. She levelled her gun. It was a relief just to see the expression on the woman's face change.

Another wave. Lota turned and ran; she didn't care where now and it seemed almost by accident that she wound up facing the minister's door.

But there was Verbal.

Lota's stomach lurched. So she hadn't dreamed it. He was slumped forward, against a chair—directly opposite the dead man. In the time she'd been gone the hourglass had spread itself and darkened; it now covered almost the entirety of his lower back.

"What the hell happened?"

Verbal didn't respond.

"*What happened?*" Lota leaned in, pressing her hands against Verbal's shoulders. He collapsed heavily against her, and—though she tried to steady him—in another moment his weight propelled them both to the floor.

When Lota got up again, she saw that the front of her shirt was covered with blood. She touched the blood with the fingers of one hand, then looked at them. Verbal looked at them, too. They sat there for a moment, looking at the blood on her hand.

"He—he had a gun," Verbal said. "And . . . and you." It was painful to look at him. "You," he said, "you were coming in behind."

Lota grabbed his shoulders again. Shook him. "So?" she screamed. "So what?"

"He had a gun," Verbal repeated. "I didn't want . . ."

Lota sobbed. She shook Verbal's shoulders, but more gently now. "So what? So what?" she cried. But by now only the light parts of Verbal's eyes were visible. They were nothing but surfaces—practically opaque. Lota scrambled to her feet; her legs felt like someone else's beneath her.

"I'll get help," she said. She moved toward the door, which was still half-open. She walked through it. There was nothing to stop her.

For the first time, she became aware of how quiet everything had become. She heard a few scattered shouts, the screeching somewhere of shoes on tile, but it all seemed to be coming from very far away, as if it had happened a long time ago.

She thought of her grandfather, who'd been a cableman. Of the stories he told: how you could sometimes hear voices, how the ghosts of old messages, long sent, still sometimes whispered through the wires.

Lota shook her head and tried to think. She glanced down at her watch but didn't fully register the time.

In any case, it was clear from the relative quiet that the guards had been disarmed, the hostages secured. Kurtz would be down in the lobby, waiting.

For her. For Verbal.

Lota needed to reach Kurtz. To tell her . . .

She hesitated. Tell her what? What, Lota wondered, her throat constricting and her mouth going suddenly dry, would she, *could* she, possibly say?

She felt for her phone in her pocket. She should have it out by now—should have already pressed Dial. Yes, in another version of this story (a version she knew better than this one, because—unlike what was happening now—it had happened so many times before), she'd already put in the call. Norm had already picked up the phone at the depot: "Everything's been secured," she'd already said. "Move out."

Again, Lota glanced down at her watch. Again, she failed to register the time.

She began to move, unsteadily, down the stairs. It was difficult going. Like plodding through waist-high water.

Just as she'd anticipated, Kurtz was waiting—her face tense, but absolutely blank. She was not looking at Lota, exactly, but past her—at the staircase Lota was descending, the exact point where the steps disappeared, spiralling toward the upper floors.

Lota opened her mouth to speak. She pulled the phone from her pocket and extended it toward Kurtz. She didn't know what to do with it now and didn't want it in her hand.

Kurtz only continued to look past Lota toward the point where the steps gave way, revealing their overall structure.

Norma was there and, for once, her eyes were visible. She, too, was looking at Lota strangely—an odd little grin beginning at the corners of her lips. Bruno opened the front door slightly. Light streamed suddenly in.

Confused, Lota closed her mouth. *They don't know*, she thought. She'd simply assumed . . . with the shots, the commotion, the long delay . . .

She looked down. Saw Verbal's blood on her shirt, her hand.

It didn't make sense. They *had* to know. There could be no mistake . . . And yet still Kurtz had said nothing. Still Bruno had opened the embassy door and let the light stream in.

"Verbal—" Lota managed. But Kurtz had already stepped forward. She raised her hand in front of her face, as if to protect herself from a physical blow.

So, it was understood after all; she would not be required to explain. Still holding the phone out toward Kurtz, she descended the last few steps in silence.

"Everything *secure*?" Kurtz said. She enunciated each syllable unnaturally.

Lota looked from Kurtz to Bruno, then—propelled by something outside of herself—she retracted the phone, pressed Dial.

"Hello? Hello?" Norm's voice erupted loudly. "What the hell's happening down there?"

Bruno was still holding the door open, letting in the heat and the light from the street.

"Hello! Goddammit, hello!" Norm was shouting. Lota looked at Kurtz again. For a brief but extraordinary moment, she thought she saw a flicker of something like doubt cross her face.

"Hello, Norm, yes," Lota said. "Everything's secure."

Kurtz turned. If she had cast a spell, it broke. Lota dropped the phone into her pocket. Bruno tossed his head, then lunged through the open door. He advanced down the path, toward the van. Kurtz followed. Then Hannibal, Joker, Norma, Alex DeLarge, and Baby Jane.

Finally Lota. She exited slowly, then practically ran down the path. The sun felt good on her skin. Purifying. For a second, she actually thought that everything was—or would be—all right. For a second, she thought they could begin again from the beginning. Pick up the dream where it had been disrupted by the first shot; reverse the direction of the hourglass stain that had spread its way both up and down the length of Verbal's back.

As she approached the van, she saw that a small crowd had formed on the street. They shouted at one another, or stood silent, or whispered together in little groups.

Among them was Frank Ramon, chief of police. He paced restlessly in front of his van, looking bewildered and twirling his baton. Christine stood opposite. She seemed to be explaining something.

It had been a mistake what had happened, Lota told herself firmly. That was all. Kurtz had warned them—she'd done her best. "This Army existed before you and will continue to exist long after you are gone." They'd repeated this all together, in unison. Lota herself had said the words out loud, had learned them by rote, had repeated them in dreams.

Perhaps, it occurred to her now, what had happened to Verbal—what was happening to all of them now—was a sort of punishment: for having so simply, so unthinkingly, repeated the words.

But then she caught herself. What had happened was not something that had happened to *her*, to *them*. It was just something that had happened.

The van door had been left open and Lota clambered in.

A simple mistake! That's what their lives amounted to—in the scheme of things, and after the fact . . .

The van's engine bumped, then roared.

Lota recalled Verbal's face. The way the tension had slackened between them. How the dark parts of his eyes had slipped below the white parts.

"*I'll get help*," she'd said. Then she'd walked through the door, down the stairs. Had pressed Dial. She'd stepped through the embassy door, had felt purified by the sun.

The van lurched forward. "*Turn back!*" Lota shrieked. But her mouth stayed firmly closed. No sound escaped.

It was too late. Again, she recalled the whites of Verbal's eyes. And yet—it was wrong to leave him. It was—

Don't think, Lota thought.

The engine moaned. They were climbing the only hill on the island.

This was not a time to think. Why else had they run everything through so many times in their minds? *So they didn't have to think*. So the whole thing would happen the way blinking happened, or swallowing. Or ducking your head to avoid a blow.

Later, there would be time to think. Later, there would be all the time in the world.

A pop startled her, followed by a fizzing sound. Norma had cracked open a can of soda. She took a long sip, then passed it to Joker, who passed it—with an apologetic smile—to Lota. She drank thirstily.

SIX

With the first shout, something inside Rachel stood up on end like the hair of a dog.

She'd just known, she wasn't sure how. She'd felt it; had flown to the window. But she saw nothing out of the ordinary out there. The cracked pavement of the embassy walk was deserted. The lawn looked like it had never been walked on at all. Across the street, Bo Brown staggered in a familiar pattern, on his way either to or from Josie's canteen. A white van parked on the side of the road had its door rolled back, but there didn't appear to be anyone inside.

Rachel wasn't like Ray—someone who was nearly always "sensing" something wrong when nothing was, in fact, wrong at all. She was more practical than that, and proud of it.

Ray couldn't help it, of course. He'd been brought up—as Rachel used to like to say—to "make the worst of everything."

In the beginning, she'd said it fondly; she'd loved being the one to swoop in and set things right. This was no doubt on account of her own upbringing. She'd inherited a sort of compulsive optimism and, though she claimed not to abide by any generalized *code*, it felt immoral to her not to at least believe that things were going to turn out all right. In the beginning, whenever Ray voiced his worry over what seemed, to Rachel, like the most trivial things, she would laugh. "*You!*" she'd say, touching his face. "Stop your worrying, *you*."

But then her voice would deepen slightly, in the way that it always did when she either more or less literally meant business. "First of all," she'd say, counting it off on a thumb, "it's not a *rational* response, worry. It's a leftover flight response, a residual animal instinct." It was possible that, at one time, Rachel may have enjoyed attributing residual animal instincts to Ray, but once they were married, and especially after Zoe was born, his habit of turning what seemed to her to be completely innocuous situations into potential life threats had begun to strike her as cowardly and insecure.

And yet it had been Rachel, not Ray, who'd insisted on leaving the island. In this *particular case*, she'd protested, the threat was not imagined but real. Unlike Ray, she'd always had an instinctive sense of the difference.

"You know," she'd said to him one day shortly after they met, "you can bring things on yourself if you think about them too hard." They'd been studying together for the officers' exam and he'd just betrayed himself for the first time by cataloguing all the quite-nearly-but-not-entirely-impossible ways things could go wrong. "It's like you *create* the possibility of bad things happening," she'd said seriously, "just by thinking that they might." Then, having sensed she'd veered embarrassingly toward the metaphysical, she'd corrected herself by adding: "It's been scientifically proven. There's all these studies on negative thinking. You can actually measure the effects."

After Zoe was born—when real threats began, for both of them, to take on a more definite shape—Rachel had found herself less and less tolerant of Ray's imagined ones. She reminded him often that even infants "absorbed everything"; they both needed to be careful, she said, if they didn't want Zoe to grow up as Ray had—afraid of every little thing.

Ray didn't ever argue, exactly. Not even during those incredibly stressful months when Rachel's own, very real worry had driven them all nearly over the brink. His strategy was instead to turn her words against her. "But why *create* these possibilities, Rachel?" he'd said to her just last week, for example, when Rachel—despite her better judgment—had expressed concern over the future of both their careers. "Why project yourself like that into a future you actively hope will never arrive?"

Rachel hadn't let him gloat for long. "Oh let's not pretend this is suddenly *my* problem," she'd said.

Later, though, unable to let the subject drop, she added: "But I wonder if there isn't, after all, in your *own* worry and projection, some sort of perverse desire for the shit to really hit the fan? You know, fire and brimstone and all that. Yes. *Maybe . . .*" (Her voice had quickened slightly; now that the ball was in her court again, she was beginning to have a little fun.) "Maybe you haven't got quite as far away from all that as both of us would like to suppose. Maybe, deep down, you're still waiting for everything—and every*one*—to quite literally go to hell!"

This time Ray went so silent on the other end of the line that it wasn't even silence anymore.

"Ray!" she had shouted after a thunderous moment or two. "Ray, come *on*! I'm joking!"

Of course she'd been joking. And yet for some reason her words came back to her now as she stood staring out the window of her third-floor office at the absolutely-nothing that was happening outside.

There was another shout. A door banged. Rachel heard a clatter of heavy footsteps on the stairs.

Maybe it was she and not Ray who'd been waiting for the shit to really hit the fan—and maybe this was it (her heart collided with the back of her chest): the thing that, without even knowing it, she'd been waiting for.

She grabbed the heavy receiver of the office phone. It was halfway to her ear before she wondered who on earth she was going to call. The ambassador's office was just a few doors from her own; she could be there in fifteen seconds if she wished to speak to him.

But what good would it do to speak to the ambassador?

A series of muffled screams reverberated in the hall. Every one of Rachel's nerves stood up on end. She dialed headquarters. If the decision turned out to be rash, she counselled herself as she pushed the buttons on her phone, she could certainly not be blamed at this point for jumping to conclusions.

But another shout interrupted these thoughts, and in the same moment the ringing stopped; the line clicked.

"Hello?" she said. Because of the shout she'd missed the "hello" from the other end and was at first not altogether certain if there was actually anyone on the line.

"Yes," the response came. "Hello? Hello?"

"Hello!" Rachel almost shouted. She was so relieved at having made contact with someone—anyone—that for a full second or two she was unable to speak.

"Yes—hello. Can I help you?"

"Yes, yes, *thank you*," Rachel finally managed. "I'm not sure if you're already aware—" (Why did she feel the need to make room for the possibility that it was she who was ignorant or mistaken, not the person she addressed?)

The clatter of footsteps on the stairs had grown louder. They'd reached the third floor. She could hear them pounding almost directly outside of her door.

"Who am I speaking with?"

"Rachel," Rachel hissed. Her heart was beating so quickly now that it felt as if her rib cage might explode. "Rachel Darling. I'm reporting what appears to be a sort of—general attack. I'm not exactly sure of the nature, but if you could please alert—"

A shot. *Jesus.* Coming from—where? Not far, certainly. Rachel had felt it rather than heard it. Next door, even? Could it have been that close?

"Ma'am? Mrs. . . . Darling? Ma'am?"

"An attack!" Rachel said. Her voice was nearly strangled now, with impatience and fear. "There's—there's shots being fired!"

Two more shots rang out then in such quick succession that Rachel didn't hear the response from whomever it was she was speaking to. The door opened and a young woman in a football jersey burst in. She was bug-eyed, scrawny. She looked like an addict, Rachel thought. Except that her eyes, rather than glazed and dull-seeming, were steady and hard. But it was strange. The girl was standing directly in front of Rachel, looking right at her, and it was as if she didn't even see her. Was it possible, Rachel wondered, that she was somehow invisible to the girl? Was it possible—

But then she saw something flicker in the girl's eye. She saw the girl's hand drift toward her belt; saw her raise a gun . . .

"*Shut up!*" the girl screamed. Though no one had spoken.

Her head loomed strangely. Rachel looked at the gun. It was, she noticed, cocked at a slight angle. If it was trained on anything, it was on something behind and above Rachel rather than on Rachel herself. This seeming carelessness comforted her and she suddenly saw what was happening for what it was: a ridiculous bit of theatre, conducted by amateurs. Yes, it was of at least some comfort to Rachel to realize that, if this was the shit hitting the fan, it wasn't going to be professional about it.

The realization did nothing, of course, to change the fact that a gun was being pointed, even if generally, in her direction, but now, at least, the young woman's face had regained its normal proportions.

"Put the phone down!"

Rachel followed the girl's gaze. The phone in her hand felt utterly remote to her now and, more because of this than the girl's order, she dropped it. It made a sick, cracking sound as it made contact with the floor.

Even the fact that the girl was wielding a gun, for example, Rachel thought, indicated that she understood what she was up against—and who was ultimately in control. How, after all, Rachel wondered, could anyone, even for a moment, imagine they might be able to get away with this sort of thing?

And what was "this sort of thing," anyway? Rachel studied the young woman's face without being able to read its expression. What was she looking for? What did she think she stood to *gain*? And where—after she'd gained it—did she imagine she could hide?

If you followed the one main road on the island south it took you through town and deposited you at the fishing wharf. A few commercial trawlers bobbed lazily there; old men dropped lines, kids passed cigarettes or leapt carelessly off the end of the pier. If you followed it in the other direction, the road gave way to a dirt track about a quarter mile past the depot. In another mile, it ended abruptly at the gated entrance to Ø Com's outer station. The station was unvisited even by most Ø Com staff, surrounded by concrete and barbed wire.

For a moment Rachel almost felt sorry for the girl. She must know, even now, that whatever she thought she was doing was over even before it had begun. That it was only a matter of time before the Empire swooped in to settle the whole thing.

The girl steadied her aim; Rachel's confidence wavered. It occurred to her how very far away the island was from the capital. How long it would take for anyone to reach them.

With a jolt, she recalled a conversation she'd had with Phil Mercer shortly after she'd arrived. "Who's to say," Phil had said, "we don't wake up tomorrow and the army's taken over the cable?"

"But the island doesn't have an army," Rachel informed him.

"Right." Phil grinned. "The police, then."

Rachel looked back at him blankly.

"Well, someone with guns. Someone on this island has got to have guns," Phil said. "And someone with guns—you'll agree with me—could at least *potentially* take over the cable . . ."

Rachel had frowned at this skeptically—but nodded.

Phil let out a short loud laugh. "Well, if anyone ever tried anything like that . . ." he said and wiped the sweat that had begun to bead on his forehead with the back of his hand. "They wouldn't, of course," he added, "but if *they did*—if anyone ever broke into the main station and held the cable hostage or something crazy like that . . ." He flicked his wrist so that the sweat he'd collected spattered—a small but perceptible drop landing on the end of Rachel's nose. "It wouldn't," he concluded with a shrug, "actually be that big a deal."

The main station, Phil had gone on to explain, these days functioned primarily as a decoy. A few old connections still ran through it—local stuff only; nothing beyond the Pacific reef. It was the outer station, built in the mid-2000s, that now served as the access point for all the trans-Pacific lines.

When Rachel had visited the main station during the first week or so of her stay, it had still looked and felt like a big deal to *her.* There'd been a video monitor and a couple of stony-faced armed guards at the gate, and the technicians inside were always, apparently, on high alert. They spent the entire length of Rachel's visit running back and forth between flashing red lights, though the young tech who toured her assured her that nothing was actually wrong.

"An alarm is a symptom," he'd said, "an indication of a failed connection. It doesn't indicate what caused the failure, though, and most of the time it isn't anything very severe."

The outer station eliminated this sort of guesswork, Phil told Rachel later. With the old station—because no single person understood the entire system—they'd been constantly either trying to prevent or recover from human error. But the new system (Phil winked), it understood itself! It solved its own problems—took efficiency to a whole new level.

"Well, *no*," he'd admitted when Rachel pressed him, the station wasn't, despite the rumours, entirely unmanned. Or at least it wasn't *yet*. The planes Rachel had noticed taking off and landing at odd hours at the island's north end were international specialists, he said. The system was just like any other computer system; it needed constant updating.

The blinds had not been drawn and Rachel squinted against the glare. The barrel end of the young woman's gun came into sharp focus as she did so. For a brief, unsettling moment, Rachel felt as though she could see down its whole length.

Well, in any case, she thought, even if Phil's unlikely fantasy was actually coming true and the young woman was after the cable, she was clearly no specialist. She probably had no idea that the main station handled only local traffic, that it consisted of only a few of the most inessential wires . . .

No, Rachel thought as she stared down the barrel of the girl's gun, even if this bunch *was* after the cable, it was quite certain that they weren't going to get very far. The thought impressed her. It was remarkable, she considered, how calm she'd managed to remain. Despite how many times she'd argued that mere anxiety was neither a rational nor a worthwhile response to real or imagined danger, she would hardly have expected herself to react this way—or to remain so confident that it was the young woman, *not* her, who stood at that moment on the losing end of the gun.

The tension between them was as taut as a wire. Rachel was conscious of how it held them both—equally—in check; how restricted they were by the opposition between the brute force of single moments and the tedious cruelty of history; how, for both of them—in that particular, shared, instance—there was nothing to gain, as well as nowhere to retreat, nowhere to go.

But then the young woman stepped forward. The gun was, very definitely, pointed at Rachel now and the balance was thrown. Rachel felt only her utter inequivalence—and the absolute emptiness of her own hands.

She tried to dismiss the feeling, tried to regain the cool confidence she'd felt just moments before, but it was hard. Really, she told herself firmly, she'd done everything she possibly could—and at significant personal risk—in alerting the capital. There was no use dwelling on what she might have done otherwise, or on what would happen now. Besides, every practical consideration of the matter led her to the same conclusion: it was only a matter of time. Help *would* arrive—was even now on its way.

Yes, Rachel thought a little desperately, all of this would soon be no more than a brief, skewed memory—a titillating anecdote, or a half-remembered dream.

She even felt a flicker of pleasure at the thought of recounting the story at some future date. She could just see Ray—mouth open, eyes wide—a caricature, almost, of disbelief and genuine alarm.

He'd ask her to repeat the story endlessly after that—and to practically everyone they met. "Oh, and Rachel's last week on the island was *eventful*, wasn't it? Rachel—tell." Rachel would be obliged to revisit the incident often—the story inevitably changing a little each time it got told. Ray would correct her sometimes, chiming in with the details—sometimes even fully taking over in order to tell it "properly" himself.

She hoped she was not already forgetting anything that would come in handy later. She cast back, but her mind felt blurry.

The shout, she thought. She needed to remember the shout. And the footsteps. The number of shots fired. She needed to remember the quiet, weirdly intimate moment she'd shared with the young woman—both of them held in check, equally, by the impossibility of executing their own power.

And how, for a moment, she'd nearly felt sorry for her. "Yes," she would say to Ray. "I quite honestly did. I mean, if you really think about it. If you think about the absolute *desperation* involved in embarking on something of that sort—something so obviously, and from the outset, *doomed* to fail . . .

"And you know the sorriest thing," she'd say on another occasion—out to dinner, this time, with friends. "The sorriest thing is that there's absolutely *nothing* one can *do*."

The conversation would proceed from there, beginning with the relative value of mediation and the possibilities of restorative justice, until at last they would all unhappily agree that the island's biggest mistake had been its failure to recognize that it had already been lost.

Yes, it had been a mistake (they all "hated to say") to resurrect the island in the first place—a mistake to have imagined it could have been simply reconstructed out of mortar and sand, the introduction of invasive, non-native species, and a hasty financial plan assembled from unsustainable sources. It had been a mistake to believe that a balance could be restored between the future and the past, when (just as Phil Mercer had said at the last meeting Rachel had attended with the Ø Com advisory board) "there's only ever one way forward, every time."

Phil had been sipping coffee from an insulated mug and jabbing at a map with his free hand. "If you draw a line from one coast to the next," Phil said—his eyes darting between Rachel and the ambassador—"we're smack dab in the centre every time. The future is us" (jab). "And it's here" (jab). "And it's *now*."

The young woman lunged toward Rachel. Rachel closed her eyes. She felt the pressure of hard metal, then heard a sharp click.

"Wait!"

The sound of her own voice surprised her. She wondered why it was the first time it had occurred to her to speak out loud.

She opened her eyes. "I'm not at all sure what's going on here," she said, looking around, "but I can assure you, there's going to be a whole lot of trouble if . . ."

Unfortunately, she sounded less like a first secretary who'd suddenly remembered that she was in charge and more like an exasperated mother—accustomed to being trampled upon.

The young woman yanked hard on the metal chain of the handcuffs. The sharp edges of the cuff dug into Rachel's skin; her knees buckled.

"Get down," the girl hissed.

"All right," Rachel said weakly. She was already down.

But then, because she couldn't help herself: "I'm telling you, though. You're going to be sorry."

The girl clicked the empty cuff open, threaded the chain behind the desk's top drawer handle, then shut the cuff on Rachel's free hand. Her wrists were pressed together now, her arms yanked up around her ears.

The girl's gun was askew again, Rachel noticed, pointed somewhere between the window and the filing cabinet. But the way she was looking at Rachel, she might as well have had it pointed directly between her eyes. Whatever depth Rachel had detected in her before—a flicker of fear, or at least of uncertainty—was gone. She was nothing but surfaces now.

Rachel's throat felt dry; she almost choked. She'd been stupid, she realized. Why couldn't she have kept her big mouth shut? Why couldn't she have just . . . played along?

But then the girl stepped back abruptly. Her eyes widened. She lowered her gun.

How much time had passed now? One hour? Three? It was impossible to tell. The way her arms were positioned, Rachel could see only the bottom corner of her watch. She'd have to wait until at least twenty past four before she'd know the time.

Of course, by then, all of this would be over. Surely, Rachel thought, her message had been received. Surely, immediate action had been ordered—the military police mobilized.

No doubt, she reasoned, time was passing for her much slower than it actually was. But still . . .

Again, Rachel strained to look at her watch, but neither the long hand nor the short hand was visible to her. She tried counting to sixty—just to remind herself how slow a minute could feel—but she got distracted before she even reached twenty-five.

Surely by now, though, at least an hour had passed . . . twice the time it would take a plane to . . .

But then, of course, they'd need time to assess the situation, to make a plan . . . And in the meantime?

Rachel yanked hard with her bound wrists against the desk drawer. The flesh smarted; she choked back a yell.

But it was a relief, she found, to begin to feel angry, rather than either smug or scared. Again she yanked against the desk —taking some pleasure this time in the way it made her wrists burn. Where *was* everyone? What was *taking* so long?

She took a deep breath, tried to calm herself. She simply had to wait. Could not permit herself to let her imagination get the better of her.

Pleased with the effect of such a reasonable train of thought, Rachel reflected that one really *did* achieve a different perspective on things when forced into such a difficult situation. She would tell Ray that. "Everything comes into focus," she'd say. "It sounds like a cliché, but it really does. You can't help but start to see things differently, to understand what *matters*."

It's not like memorizing the Operations Handbook, she'd add, or calculating known risks, or signing a waiver. It's not about probability anymore—or even about possibility. It's just about what *is*. Plain and simple.

"It may even be . . ." she'd reflect, "that it's really only when you come face to face, not just with the *possibility* of death but with its absolute inevitability, that life becomes"—here she'd pause for emphasis, reach slowly across the table for Ray's hand—"*real*."

Ray's hand would feel warm and familiar. She'd stroke it slowly, feel a pulse throbbing in the thumb and the wrist. "Rules and regulations," she'd tell him, "even—or especially—the ones we learn by rote, simply no longer apply in extreme cases, it seems. There isn't any *could*, there isn't any *should* anymore."

Outside, a motor gunned. There was a whoop. A screech of tires. Rachel's thoughts scattered—her heart slammed heavily inside her chest.

What if . . . ?

The idea dawned slowly at first, but then all at once it was upon her. What if, she thought, the insurgents simply don't know what they're up against? What if they don't know that all of this—whatever "this" is—is doomed from the outset? A meaningless charade? There was, after all, no reason for them to be aware of what she herself barely knew: the extent of, and the reason behind, the island's importance as both a strategic military base and a hub for global trade. There was no reason they *shouldn't* imagine, therefore, that their little coup, or whatever it was, might pass beneath the radar. Why would anyone, they might think, kick up a fuss over what happened out here, on what was little more than a mound of reinforced concrete, adrift somewhere in the South Sea?

The thought chilled Rachel. She listened for more sounds from the street, but heard nothing. If this was not just an amateurish heist, she considered—a bunch of lunatics who'd bitten off a little more than they could chew—but people who actually believed they had a shot at something, she had a lot more to worry about than she'd originally thought.

She shifted slightly, leaning into the desk. Her mouth felt dry. She tried—and failed—to swallow.

SEVEN

The outer station had been built a year after Lota was born, and so, for as long as she could remember, it had been there, perched at the far northern tip of the island like a big dead bird. As kids they'd torn down the road on bikes only to pull up short in front of the huge metal gate with its sign that read, in black paint—more and more of which flaked away each year —"Authoriz   Person Only Bey   P nt." A few video cams were mounted on thin poles and lined the gravel drive, so they always had the uncanny feeling that they were being watched whenever they drew near.

Lota had never in her life seen anyone at, or around, the station, and the rumour was that no one ever set foot there at all.

Who, then, was watching? And why? The question had often crossed her mind, but until she met Kurtz she'd never considered it for long. Aside from the gate and the video cams, there was nothing to see except a squat concrete building at the end of the short drive, a TV or radio tower, a helicopter landing pad, and patches of overgrown Mexican creeper. It was not much to incite the curiosity even of a child.

As far as she was aware, no one knew what happened at the outer station, or if they knew, they didn't care. People badmouthed Ø Com any chance they got (every promise they'd ever made had been broken at least several times; where were the jobs? where was the new wharf? the road? the money for the hospital? the schools?), but they didn't spend a lot of time speculating about what obviously didn't concern them.

It wasn't until Kurtz pointed toward the far northern tip of the island on the map one day—the only space on the map that had been left curiously blank—and said, "That's our prize," that Lota had paid much attention.

"They want us to believe that it doesn't exist," Kurtz had said. "They want to make the cable disappear the way they made the island disappear. But nothing ever really disappears. Nothing ever just goes away. It might get hidden! It might get buried somewhere, or disguised. But *something* is always there, and *everything*"—her eyes panned the room—"depends on *something*. The price of oil, for example! The Dow Jones industrial average! The security of at least half of the major intelligence organizations on this planet! *Everything*," Kurtz said, "*depends* on a wireless system that has never actually been wireless! *We are standing*"—she raised her arms above her head and stared down at her feet, planted squarely on the basement floor—"on the last remaining land access point for one of the largest and most expensive cable systems in the entire world. In another year or two, who knows? Maybe even *this* point will be plunged underground. But for now"—she shook her head slowly—"we open the gates of the outer station and we're practically tripping over it. For now we still have a chance. We have a point of entrance, of disruption—and therefore of negotiation. Of *power*!"

"Very few people seem to get this," Lota remembered Kurtz saying once, soon after she'd joined the Army. "They say wireless, so we think wireless. They say instant, they say global, they say assets, profit, average, return. And just so long as certain bank accounts keep growing, *we believe every word!* But the thing is . . ." Kurtz lowered her voice. "The wire actually exists. It's *real*. And it's right under our noses. All we have to do is take it. Because what they *don't get*, and *we do*, is that everything's connected, that nothing comes from, or can be made from, nothing. That even what they take for granted—what they imagine is silent, or invisible, *exists* at some level—is a unit of power or meaning that can be used, transformed, or"—her lips curled at the corners, a playful, mocking expression that sent shivers running up and down Lota's spine—"*taken away*.

"But it won't be easy," she continued. "Because we're not just dealing with invisible numbers and wires. We're dealing with invisible people, too—and people, invisible or not, are far less predictable than numbers or wires." She stabbed at the blank space on the map with a clenched fist. "This," she'd said, "this. What you're looking at right now is not only the last remaining land access point for the largest and most powerful telecommunications network in the world. It's *also*"—her eyes panned the room again. She wanted to make sure they were with her; they were. As usual, they listened with the hair standing up on their necks, hardly breathing, hanging on her every word. "It's *also*," Kurtz said, "a top-secret, heavily guarded black site, home to roughly sixty-five of the Empire's most-wanted terrorist suspects, political prisoners, and other detainees."

Lota felt a disturbed flutter of something: the rustlings of a long-forgotten memory, or else a vague premonition of something she didn't understand. For a moment something very nearly took shape—but then, just as swiftly, it was gone. She pictured the gates of the outer station. The perched video cams, the scrub grass. Never once in all the countless times Lota had driven up to those gates had she seen a single sign of life.

"*Information*," Kurtz was saying. "When it comes into the station through the wire, flows right out the other end. Information that comes into the station any *other* way, by helicopter, or private plane . . . Well, let's just say, it doesn't very often come out."

Lota felt the same sensation driving through the gates of the outer station as she had sometimes jumping off the end of the wharf into the sea. There seemed to be an actual physical adjustment to a new element, or system of gravity.

What was alarming, in both cases, was how easy it was to leave the old system behind. One moment there was solid ground beneath her and the next—there was not. By the time Lota arrived at the station with Kurtz, the gates had been rolled open, the alarms and security cameras had been disabled, the dogs restrained or subdued.

It wouldn't have been so simple if, six months before, by a stroke of luck, Hal's brother, Nick, hadn't been hired on at the main station as a guard. His hire, along with the hires of two other islanders, had been announced at a community meeting. An Ø Com representative had been present—sweating through his shirt. The islanders received him as they always received outsiders: with both awe and contempt.

As usual, they wanted to hate him. There was even a scattering of hisses and boos from the crowd as the representative rose to give his short address and welcome the three new members to his staff. But they couldn't hate him—not quite. Because there was Hal's brother and two others of their own, looking awkward and pleased in their pressed uniforms. They couldn't help but feel a little grateful—and a little proud, too. In the same way, perhaps, that Lota had felt both grateful and proud the first time she'd seen her brother Marcus in uniform, when she was ten.

Marcus had been in the navy for less than three weeks, but even in that short time he'd been utterly transformed. At first, Lota had been unable even to touch him—let alone throw her arms around him or climb up his pant legs as she might have at some other time. She'd only stood there, staring shyly at him until—in a strained, embarrassed voice Lota had never heard before—her mother told her sharply to close her mouth.

Even then, Lota must have recognized in the polished shoes her brother wore, the sharply pressed lines of his jacket and pants, the earnest and, at the same time, strangely aloof quality of his gaze, what was—for her brother or for any other island boy—the only possible escape.

Because, despite the deep resentments the islanders still harboured toward the Empire, it was clear to everyone—even to Lota, at the age of ten—that without it, the island never would have existed. Clearer still was that the island's *continued* existence depended, almost solely, on the Empire's protection and goodwill. Although this fact elicited in most a complicated reaction that did not exclude blatant disgust, or even rage, island men who joined the Empire's army or navy were still proudly celebrated as valiant defenders not only of the rights and freedoms of islanders but of the rights and freedoms of all.

Working for Ø Com was not at all like working for the navy, of course, but for a moment—perhaps because Hal's brother had recently had his long hair shorn, or because of the uniforms and military-style berets—it was difficult to tell the difference.

The Ø Com man continued to speak; the crowd, by turns, to hiss and cheer. They wanted to hate him, but there was something admirable—almost noble, really—in the way he continued (chin jutted, head cocked a little to one side) to calmly deliver his speech, seemingly oblivious to the intermittent jeers and taunts. As with all white ghosts, though, if you looked closely enough, what appeared on the surface as confidence and formal reserve soon became indistinguishable from distress.

Three lousy jobs!

"And that'll do them fine, for another seventy years!" Nick and Hal's great-uncle Armand had said. He'd been sitting up front, near bursting with anger and pride, seeing as it was his own grand-nephew who'd given them all the opportunity to get so upset. "Anytime we complain they'll say, didn't we hire your boy Nick? Don't you recall, sometime not long ago, we dressed him in a uniform, gave him a gun?"

Now, though, it was precisely on account of Nick Fromm's gun that the Black Zero Army was making its way through the gates of the outer station. It was not by any accident, that is, that Nick had been on duty when Norm and Hal had driven up to the main station earlier that morning. Just as arranged, he'd promptly directed them toward the keys to the outer station and handed over his gun. By the time Lota had arrived with Kurtz and the rest of the Army, the main station was secure and Nick was standing—along with the foreign guard, the technicians, and the rest of the station personnel—with his hands bound, looking as awkward and confused as he had at the community meeting six months before.

At nearly seven feet tall, he loomed at least a head taller than everyone else and reminded Lota of the wooden totem, carved by a visiting artist a few years back, which now stood near the clock tower in the centre of town. It was "the Birdman," the visiting artist had informed them, because hardly anyone remembered the deity anymore. He represented a time before men and women were sent to live on the earth and the birds were sent to live in the sky; a time when all humans and animals were one, and everything existed as it always had in the mind of the great spirit who did not distinguish between man and animal, heaven and hell, water and sky.

Was that why the island had suffered so much? Lota had asked. Everyone turned to stare, but Lota pretended not to notice. She was standing on tiptoe, toward the back of the crowd, her arms folded protectively across her small chest. Was that why? she asked again. A muddle-headed god who couldn't keep the difference straight in his mind, who couldn't tell water from earth or good from bad?

The artist had taken off his hat and shielded his eyes against the glare of the sun. Sweat had collected in a ring around his head and now he rubbed it away. Yes, he responded uneasily. As far as he understood the story, at least, that was the reason for the suffering that now existed among all people on earth.

But Lota had continued to puzzle over the question. She'd hardly listened while the artist spoke—in more confident tones now—about the history and process of his work, and remained distracted even after the talk had ended and everyone had begun to mill about, drinking lemonade from plastic cups and helping themselves to finger sandwiches and chocolate macaroons. What the artist had said didn't make sense, she realized, and even her own question was somehow off. Because the muddle-headed god was a god from the *before-time*—a time when everything had existed in balance and human beings and animals had lived in peace. Lota half wanted to interrupt the little party to warn the artist of his mistake. It was not the *Birdman,* she wanted to say, but whoever it was who'd first torn the bodies of men from the bodies of birds, whoever had first drawn back the water from the earth and the earth from the sky. It was *he* and not the mixed-up dreaming god who'd been the cause of the people's suffering.

Nobody else seemed concerned. They chatted mildly and munched on macaroons, and slowly drifted away. Lota stayed, however, for some time after, hovering beside the refreshment table and watching the artist as he continued to work—still wondering to herself whether the figure he carved represented the cause of, or their deliverance from, suffering.

And ever since, whenever Lota saw the Birdman in the centre of town, she was reminded of the resigned and meticulous patience of the artist—as well as of his mistake. It came to seem as though, in a way, it was he who was her distant ancestor, rather than the bird.

But now it was, very certainly, the bird and not the artist that Nick Fromm resembled as he stood beside the foreign guard and technicians outside the main station. He stared at them as they drove away, bewildered. He shook his head—not in opposition or resistance, but in wonder and disbelief.

In no time at all after that they were bumping along the rough gravel drive, crowded at the edges with pigweed and creeper; in no time they were clearing the gates of the outer station and Lota was feeling the same way she did whenever she jumped off the end of the wharf into the sea.

The cameras, suspended and glinting, winked at them from their high poles. Leaning partway out the passenger window, Kurtz raised her gun at one of them and fired. The bulb spat and shattered; fine splinters of glass rained down like a sudden sun shower. She fired again. Then Mad Max, leaning out a rear window, fired. Then Baby Jane opposite. Bang. Pop. Buzz. Bang. Pop. Buzz. The cameras burst and scattered along the drive. Tiny shards of glass twinkled like fallen stars.

And still nothing happened. No alarm sounded; nothing, or nobody, appeared. Lota watched the low building and tightened her grip on her gun. Her heart pounded. She began to doubt that anything, or anyone, was actually inside the building. But the more she doubted, the more terrified she became.

Then a shot echoed loudly; they were within fifty yards of the building. Another shot followed. Then another.

Lota couldn't tell where the shots were coming from, and for a terrifying moment it seemed as though they were being fired from the earth itself, surrounding them from every side. But then Kurtz fired back and a figure stumbled, then fell, from the station's low roof. To Lota, it was as though it happened backwards. The figure was already falling before she noticed that Kurtz had raised her gun.

After that there was a deafening silence. The van screeched to a halt and Baby Jane hauled open the back door. They poured out, one after another. More guns fired. But Lota's heart no longer pounded in her chest. It seemed as if it hardly beat at all. The feeling had gone in her legs and hands, but she continued to move—as if automatically now. She was aware of her feet crunching gravel, of the steady progress she made toward the low building, of Kurtz's voice—though she couldn't make out a single word.

It didn't matter. She knew well enough what the orders were. She was to guard the entrance (she drew up abruptly in front of the door); to make sure no one either entered or exited the building; to "shoot first, ask questions later"—fire at anything and anyone that crossed her path.

"Violence," Kurtz had told them once, "is humanity recreating itself. We do not, of course, *invite* violence," she'd added very carefully, "but we do not foreclose on its possibility—or, for that matter, on any other. For the future to take place, for it to take *the* place of both the present and the past, there must be a clean break—a genuine, necessarily violent rupture."

Lota held her gun tightly and tried to swallow. Well, she considered, she was alive anyway.

The idea troubled her. She turned in circles, listened as shouts, curses, and the odd gunshot echoed from inside.

She peered into the building—saw, directly across the hall, that a set of double doors had been propped open, emptying onto a windowless room. The only light came from a door at the back. Having been left slightly ajar, it permitted a dull glow to fall in an elongated triangle along the cracked concrete floor.

Lota looked left, then right. A narrow corridor extended in both directions, tapering at the ends and glowing like an empty shell.

Doors continued to bang. Then Hal appeared. He looked different. There was something swollen about him, Lota thought. His neck looked thicker.

Behind him—shoulders thrust, mouth gagged, head wagging—was the man who, six months before, had been "honoured and proud" to welcome Nick and the two other new hires to "the Ø Com family." Norm and Hal had picked him up outside his home just as Kurtz was entering the embassy; he never went to work before ten.

Hal had him by the shoulder and led him slowly, almost tenderly, down the hall. Lota watched them approach. She swung back and forth between the corridor and the drive, and every time she swung back to the corridor they were closer than they had been before. She tried to catch Hal's eye, but there was something about them that refused to fix, or settle. It made her think of Miles. Yes, she thought—a sick feeling stirring somewhere in her gut—there was something quite definitely narcotic about the way Hal looked now.

She swung back toward the drive and scanned the horizon without really seeing anything. By the time she'd completed a full turn and stood facing the building again, Kurtz had entered the room from the back. Lota watched her through the double doors, her face plunged into shadow, her hair blazing—lit up from behind by the sliver of light.

Hal tugged the prisoner through the double doors, then stopped—quickly enough that the prisoner lurched forward, then fell. The noise that resulted—a strange scuffling—startled

Lota. She was not sure at first if it was coming from inside or outside. She turned in three complete circles, gun raised—ready.

But there was nothing but gravel outside, and Mexican creeper. Still, Lota could not be convinced. She stared at the gravel, at the weeds—swaying a little in the slight breeze. Then she whipped around again. She watched, through the open double doors, as Hal yanked the prisoner up from the floor.

Kurtz was gone now—slipped back the way she'd come. Lota was straining to peer after her when a screeching sound, like a cat being stepped on, caused her to whip around again.

Nothing. Even the weeds stood stock still.

Quickly, Lota turned back to the hall. She could still see Hal and the Ø Com man, framed by the double doors. But now, in front of them—in the exact spot where Kurtz had stood only a moment before—there swung a large metal hook. Hal took a step toward the hook, then half turned toward the Ø Com man. Lota could see his face now, the way his eyes glowed; from a distance, they appeared nearly phosphorescent.

It was possible, Lota considered hopefully, that what was happening to Hal was not, as it had first appeared to her, a sort of narcotic *distraction*, but its opposite—some of the old wisdom, returning. An apprehension of chaos as power rather than as indifference or dispersal. Yes, it was possible that, at this very moment, he was seeing right down to the particle level—past what was immediately apparent to the eye. Seeing the way that everything was both everything and nothing; identifying the buzz of chaos at the heart of all things.

But whatever it was that Hal saw at that moment, or failed to see, Lota found it difficult to look away. She forced herself to turn, to look back to the drive, but her eyes refused to focus on anything. She only stood there, blinking painfully, until the scuffling sound from inside the building distracted her again.

Hal had fastened the prisoner's handcuffs to the hook in the middle of the room and now the hook was raised; the prisoner's feet began to dance a little. He had to stand on tiptoe in order to even touch the floor.

Lota stared as the man danced—turning in little pirouetting circles. Once—briefly, and by sheer accident—she managed to catch his eye. Then his eyes flanked. He seemed to look left and right at the same time, toward both opposing walls.

Kurtz re-entered carrying a folding chair. She walked around the hanging man and set up the chair so that it faced away from Lota, toward the back of the room. Then Norma emerged; she carried a clipboard in one hand and something else in the other—perhaps a recording device.

Hal gave the prisoner a shove and he spun like a ballerina. When he stopped spinning, he faced Kurtz directly and Lota could see his eyes again. But now they weren't looking at her, or at anything, and they still seemed somehow separate, rather than a set. He had not yet made a single sound. Even when, a moment later, Hal removed the gag, the prisoner only coughed; spat a little.

Lota glanced back at the drive.

"Name, please?" (It was Kurtz who'd spoken.)

"You know me well enough."

Lota kept her eyes trained, determinedly, on the rolled-back metal gate.

"Name, please?" There was no alteration in Kurtz's tone.

A cough. An indiscernible stutter.

"Speak up, please, so the recorder can hear you."

"Philip. Philip J. Mercer."

The pull was irresistible; Lota turned back. She could see Kurtz's shoulders, rising against the back of the folding chair. The shape of her head—encircled by a fringe of hair that had been lit up by the room's single shaft of light. Beyond her, the prisoner—suspended—danced awkwardly from foot to foot.

"Do you know who I am?" Kurtz said.

The prisoner said nothing.

Kurtz extended both arms and gestured broadly, toward Hal on her left and Norma on her right. "Do you know who *we* are?"

The prisoner continued to dance. "Yes," he said. "I've been informed."

"You know our demands, then. I'm sure you'll agree. They're simple enough. And yet, I've been told you refuse to co-operate."

"Wrong!" The prisoner lurched forward, spinning on his toes. "I've told you . . . told *your people* that . . . quite the contrary. I'm very *happy* to co-operate! It's just I don't have . . . have never had, you see . . . the *precise* information you're looking for." The prisoner completed another full circle on his toes and gasped for breath. "I've got a lot of *other* information—more important information—if you're willing to listen . . ." He was losing momentum, couldn't complete another turn, and swung back, instead, the other way. "Information that can help us both! This situation . . . really," he sputtered; he seemed to be losing the thread. "What I want to say is. It puts us all at an advantage. If we could only work together."

"Let's calm down," Kurtz interrupted. "Please. Can we calm down a moment?"

The prisoner snorted. An arc of snot flew through the air and disappeared into the shadows.

"We're interested," Kurtz continued coolly, "we're *very* interested in working together. Of course. But right now you *must understand* we happen to have a pressing priority. We need the code to the system. The system owned and operated by Ø, the company for which you personally serve as the chief information officer." Kurtz paused. Only the tip-tip-tap of the prisoner's shoes could be heard in the silence. "But you," Kurtz continued, "you, the chief *information* officer, claim that you do not *have access* to this code. Put yourself in our shoes for a second, please. Would you believe *yourself*, if you were us?"

The prisoner had stopped spinning. His feet tapped insistently, in order to keep himself in place. "The operation of this system," he replied slowly, "has nothing . . . to do with me. This *place*"—he spat out the word like a tooth—"has nothing to do with me. With us. That must be obvious, even to you! Since when," he spat, "do telecommunications companies detain international criminals? You can see for yourself . . . There've been certain compromises. There've been . . ."

Another short screech interrupted the prisoner. As if on cue, he began to dance again—only now there was nothing for him to dance on. The prisoner's feet were suspended an inch or so above the floor. He howled. For a moment it was impossible to hear anything at all above the noise.

"I'm sure you'll agree," Kurtz said when he was quiet again, "it will be easier on all of us if you simply give us the information we need."

"I-don't-know-the-code!" the prisoner shouted. "I promise you, I don't. I'm just a—an HR guy, at the end of the day. I promise you. I have nothing to do with the code. I have nothing to do with the *actual system*!"

Hal took a step toward the prisoner. He removed a police baton from his back pocket and hit the prisoner once with it, just above the hip. He did not hit hard, but the impact caused the prisoner to spin first one way, and then the other—and, again, to howl.

When he stopped spinning he stopped howling. "Look," he said in a tired voice, as if he'd suddenly grown terribly bored. "I work for Ø, yes. But who, do you wonder, is Ø working for? Go ask your friends at the embassy!" He jerked his head strangely. "I've got nothing! Nothing! I promise you. Which is why . . . why I'm telling you"—his voice rose, became a strangled cry, then levelled itself again—"I *want* to work with you, I honestly do. I think the two of us"—his eyes had focused again, were fixed directly on Kurtz—"have more in common than you might think. That we could, in fact, get on very well. After all, we both want . . . what?" Again, his head jerked strangely. "A certain amount of autonomy. A certain amount of independence . . . The right to pursue our own interests. Isn't that right? Our own ends?"

There was a long pause. Then a creaking sound; the prisoner was being lowered gradually. When he hit the floor, his legs buckled. At first, he was unable to stand. Then something in him seemed to settle. He regained his balance; his head stopped twitching.

"I want you to understand something," Kurtz said. "If we *don't* manage to get the code from you . . . or from your friends at the embassy—"

"They're *not* my friends."

"—if we *don't* manage to get the code," Kurtz repeated, "from you or from your *friends*, you know we'll find some other way. You know we can simply cut the wire."

The prisoner's knees buckled again. His eyes flanked. "No!" he burst out. "No, that would be bad—*very* bad—for everyone! I don't think you quite understand."

Kurtz laughed. "Oh," she said, "but I *do*! It *would* be bad—very bad, indeed. For those, that is, who have something to lose."

"Work with me!" the prisoner begged. "I don't know the code, but I do know . . . *other* things. And I don't want to work with Vollman—*or* the Empire—any more than you do! What you said just now, see, if we work together, it's just not true. On the contrary, you and I more than anyone right now have something to lose. As well as something, potentially, to *gain*."

There was another long pause. Kurtz shifted in her seat, motioned to someone—Norma or Hal. "All right," she said finally. "So what *do* you know?"

"There are *maps*," the prisoner said.

Kurtz shrugged. "Okay. Maps."

"Thirteen terabytes' worth of side-scan sonar data," the prisoner said, more urgently. "A complete chart of the seafloor from here to each coast. The work was all commissioned by the Empire. Military operations. All highly confidential. The charts were never intended for us. It took years for us to convince them of any connection between our work and theirs. We can use those maps, I told them. If we work together, we can take our cables where no one's ever gone, chart a whole new course across the Pacific, reduce the time it takes to transmit information from coast to coast *by more than half*! It took a while, but we got there. Did we ever! At this point, even the president has a personal investment in the project. And we were all set to move forward with it until . . ." The prisoner was beginning to relax. He swung his neck as he spoke, as though addressing a large audience. "Vollman. He speaks up. For once in his life he speaks up. Doesn't want to give the land base up, he says. And the Empire, you know . . . They're attempting to *negotiate*!" Spit flew from the corners of his mouth and hung suspended for a moment, glistening. "I've tried to talk to Vollman myself. Tried to make him see. I've told him, We keep going like this, we both lose, but he doesn't listen, doesn't seem to understand."

Hal stepped forward, his baton raised. "We need the code."

The prisoner reeled back. "No!" he cried. "You don't! You just *think* you need the code! What you need"—his voice adjusted to a more reasonable note—"is to get your hands on those charts. If you managed that—I promise you—you'd have a whole lot more than access to the *existing* cable. You'd be holding—and I'm not exaggerating—the entire *future* in your hands!"

Hal took another step. The prisoner's body went rigid and both eyes shut tight. "But that's not all!" he exclaimed, still bracing himself against the expected blow.

"What we all need," Kurtz said flatly, "is to calm down."

The prisoner opened a single eye. "They try," he began again, more tentatively now, "to cover their tracks. Everything's abstract when it comes to this sort of business." Both eyes were open now. The prisoner began to wag his head suggestively and, with his bound hands, he gestured in a general sort of way around the room. "This isn't," he said, "even Empire soil. Everything's remote now, right? *Everything's someone else's business*. Impossible to track down, impossible to prove. But even so, let me tell you, they keep impeccable records."

Kurtz motioned to Hal, who stepped back. The prisoner relaxed. Then Norma leaned in. She consulted briefly with Kurtz, then walked quickly toward the double doors.

Startled to attention, Lota whipped back to the drive. It had been some time since she'd been able to train her attention on anything but the prisoner and Kurtz, and her heart beat fiercely at the thought of how much she might have failed to notice in all that time.

But there was no detectable movement outside and, relieved, Lota turned back to the hall. She glanced first right, then left, and, from that direction, could just make out Bruno headed down the corridor, four or five ghosts trailing behind.

They must be foreign technicians, Lota guessed as they drew nearer—or guards. Their hands and feet had been shackled. Baby Jane took up the rear.

Norma had reached the double doors. She kicked the doorstops out from under them and they shut slowly. At the exact moment that the doors clicked into place, the prisoner began to howl.

Lota winced and turned back toward the drive. By the time she'd swung around again, Bruno had reached the double doors. He stood there, nose in the air, the slack skin beneath his chin quivering.

"These ones are next," he said, nodding to Lota and gesturing toward the ghosts—all of whom had, by now, stumbled to a halt behind. "Make sure they don't go anywhere."

Lota stared at the ghosts and listened to Bruno's heavy footsteps retreating slowly down the hall.

"I hope you know who you're working for."

Lota blinked. Even with how she was looking right at them, she couldn't tell which one of the ghosts had spoken—or if anyone had spoken at all. Baby Jane, at the end of the single-file line, continued to pace the hall slowly; she did not appear to have heard anything.

"I worked with her, you know." The voice was harsh, unsteady, little more than a hiss. Lota turned away. She focused as far as she could down the drive, thinking maybe if she fixed on something in the distance . . .

But then she turned back. One of the ghosts was looking straight at her.

"With *that woman*," the ghost said. "Your boss. What does she call herself?"

Lota shook her head. She found it impossible now to glance away.

"She went by Santos then," the ghost said. "I forget the first name. Everybody called her the Saint. It was a joke, see, because—"

Baby Jane stood in front of the ghost; was half a head or so taller than him, was practically breathing down his throat.

The ghost continued to stare past her, but his voice sounded increasingly strained.

"She was difficult to read. A closed book."

Lota craned her neck toward the drive. Behind the closed doors, the prisoner began to scream in spasmodic bursts.

"Shut the fuck up," said Baby Jane.

"But she was smart," the ghost hissed, as if he hadn't heard. "Could get almost anyone to talk. A bit of a psycho that way. Everybody knew."

Baby Jane leaned in so that her face was practically pressed up against the ghost's own. She'd moved her hand to her gun. "I said, Shut. The. Fuck. Up!"

The latch clicked. Hal pulled one of the double doors open just wide enough to stick his head outside. "Everything all right?"

Baby Jane stepped back. Lota turned—heart pounding—toward the drive. The fence looked wobbly in the distance. She grabbed at the door frame; couldn't tell what was solid.

EIGHT

Rachel had no idea what time it was—only that it was not yet four-thirty because the short hand had not yet appeared in the bottom third of her watch.

Time had a way of playing tricks on you. It was quite possible that not quite so much time had passed as it seemed. Still, Rachel regretted not having kept track of how many times the long hand had appeared and disappeared from the bottom corner of her watch. If she had, she would at least have been able to gauge the hour.

The door opened. *Surely,* Rachel thought . . . Surely *now.* She held her breath. A young man entered. He wore khaki pants too large for him and a semi-automatic weapon slung over one arm.

"All right?"

Rachel had never been more disappointed. She exhaled loudly. The kid dragged a chair from behind the door and sat down. He slumped forward and looked at Rachel blankly. Then, as if suddenly inspired, he took a stick of gum out of one of his deep pants pockets and thoughtfully folded it into his mouth.

He tipped the pack toward Rachel. “Gum?”

Rachel shook her head.

The kid reached into his pocket again, this time retrieving a small spiral-bound notebook and a pen. He scribbled on the cover of the notebook to get the ink flowing, then flipped it open randomly to a blank, lined page.

“Name?” he said, without looking up.

Rachel was silent.

“What’s your name?” the kid repeated. He lifted his forehead slightly this time, but he kept his eyes on the page.

Rachel’s throat felt permanently closed. If she could just get a drink of water—

The kid had looked up. He was staring at her, a stupid grin on his face. “What’s that?” he said. “You don’t have a name?”

Again Rachel shook her head. She was terribly thirsty.

The kid stared. He chewed his gum slowly. “What’s—” he began again.

“Rachel!” Rachel said, croaking on the word. She cleared her throat. “Rachel Darling.”

The kid continued to chew. With every bite, the white gum flashed visibly.

“What’s yours?”

“Mine?” the kid asked.

Rachel nodded.

“Alien.”

“What?”

“You heard me.”

Rachel hadn't noticed how tense she'd been. Her back ached; her neck—craned backward and sideways, away from the desk—was killing her. She leaned forward and shook her head. Was this some sort of elaborate joke? She'd been taking everything so . . . so seriously! When now, all of a sudden, it seemed perfectly clear . . . It was all . . . a joke. A dream!

Yes, that was it. *A dream*. She nearly laughed out loud.

But then the laugh caught—the thought faltered.

If it *was* just a dream, why, Rachel wondered—now that she'd realized as much—did she go on dreaming?

She yanked hard against the desk, felt the sharp bite of metal, the wrenching pressure of the drawer as, having slid out as far as it could along its metal tracks, it met its limit. The kid was looking at her, still flashing—at semi-regular intervals—his little ball of hard white gum.

A bubble of panic rose in Rachel's throat. Why didn't she wake up, dammit? Why didn't the kid *disappear*? It made no sense, any of it, and yet, unlike in a dream, realizing this changed nothing. The kid continued to stare. Rachel's wrists to smart painfully. The drawer to extend itself from the desk only so far—to wobble stubbornly against its metal hinge.

"Tell me," the kid said, slumping still further in his chair, "what exactly do you do here?" The gun on his shoulder shifted slightly as he moved, so that now—without his even realizing it—it was pointed almost directly at Rachel.

"Do?" Rachel shook her head. She had to keep things in perspective, had to keep—over whatever it was that was happening—some degree of control. She cleared her throat loudly, levelled her gaze at the kid—and the gun. "Listen," she said. "I've a right to know. What's this all about?"

The kid looked genuinely surprised.

"I mean . . ." Rachel licked her lips, which were exceedingly dry. "Is this some sort of . . . *interrogation*?"

The kid nodded seriously, considering. He stretched his gum into a thin strand until it broke over his tongue.

"I mean," Rachel said again, and yanked impatiently against the drawer. "I *mean*," she repeated a third time, her voice rising now, almost to a whine, "you can't, you can't be . . . *serious*!"

The kid burst out laughing. He laughed for a good minute or more. A strange, strangled-sounding laugh that confused Rachel. She kept a sort of half smile playing at her own lips because of it; didn't want it to seem to the kid that she didn't get the joke, if that's what it was.

But then, as abruptly as the kid had started laughing, he stopped. He got up, stretched, and loped over to the window—leaning out over the ledge to get a wider view.

"So, this is what you see up here," he said. He started to laugh again. "Ha ha! So this is what you see! You know"—he turned to face Rachel—"it isn't really that different from what you can see from the street." He sounded neither disappointed nor surprised. The kid sat down. "We're very serious," he said as he adjusted the strap of his gun, which had begun to slip off his shoulder again. "You don't have to worry about that."

Rachel shivered, though she didn't feel cold. She had to be careful, she reminded herself. Even if this *was* a dream, its limits and therefore its consequences seemed to be real. She wondered briefly where the kid had come from—which side of the island—and if she'd seen him before. She didn't think so, but then, she had trouble keeping the island people straight in her mind. It wasn't a race thing—clearly. It was a side effect of diplomacy. It was her job to introduce herself to and shake the hands of lots of people she had no personal interest in meeting and was never going to see again. It did something to the brain. She had a tremendous capacity for remembering names and faces in the short term, but little to no capacity for lasting impressions. People blurred together in her mind—the people she met today, for example, to a certain extent interchangeable with the people she'd met yesterday or even five years before. Just watch, Rachel thought, a year from now, even this kid's face would blur and change, become confused in her mind with a dozen or so others . . .

Once again, the utter absurdity of her situation—even, or especially, if it was real—hit her.

"But you can't," she cried out, "you just can't *do this*!" She sprang forward—causing the desk drawer to slide back along its tracks and then to snap, with an efficient click, into position. "You can't just walk in here, just . . . take over like this!" It was probably imprudent to say more, but Rachel suddenly felt a petty, almost vindictive desire to counter the kid's smugness with her own. "Plus," she continued, "they *know*, you know." She nodded, for some reason, in the direction of the window. "I knew something was wrong, before anyone even came in here. I put in a call to the capital."

Her confidence had reached its peak; it had nowhere to go from there. "I reported *exactly* what's going on here," Rachel said, her voice beginning to tremble. "So there can't . . . there can't be any mistake." Her pulse was distracting; it beat loudly in her ears. She was no longer entirely sure what she was talking about.

The kid shrugged. It was an irritating gesture, which served to calm Rachel somehow. She felt annoyed rather than afraid, first with the kid and then with herself—then at the stupidity of blind luck. If only all this had happened *next* week, she thought, or even tomorrow, rather than today! If only she'd left the island in November—had *insisted*, in keeping with her instinct and better judgment; had simply said, as she'd intended, "*No.* The situation is untenable . . ."

Instead, she'd tried to please, had tried not to ruffle any feathers.

Well, now look where it had got her.

Rachel shuddered. Goddammit; she'd *known.* Ever since—at least—the incident of the dog bite, she'd *known.* She could have changed her mind then, told the ambassador she couldn't stay—told him that something else would need to be arranged. But she'd done nothing—had pressed all of their luck, had even experienced a degree of pleasure in being able to be the reasonable one; to insist to Ray that it only *made sense* to stay, that everything was going to *be all right*.

The incident had happened on a Thursday. Ray and Zoe were due to fly out the very next week. Ray had picked up Zoe from school that afternoon. She had, he said afterward, seemed unusually upbeat. They'd made a stop at the only semi-decent bakery on the island, across from the Birdman statue in the centre of town. Ray said he remembered his attention had been caught, briefly, by a group of kids huddled around the fountain; that he'd felt uneasy in a way he didn't understand.

They left the bakery and moved toward the fountain. The uneasy feeling grew. But then Rachel had called. The two of them had spoken for a minute or two, annoyed with each other for some reason (afterward, neither one of them could recall about what).

Rachel gritted her teeth. She yanked again, hard, against the drawer. It slid out as far as it could before roughly bouncing to a halt. The kid watched her from his chair, snapping his gum and shaking his head.

The truth was, Rachel thought angrily as she shook out her wrists and cursed under her breath, she'd known nothing. What was knowledge, after all—after the fact, and unaccompanied by any form of action—except the basest and most rudimentary fear? What she'd felt after the incident of the dog bite was likely nothing more complicated than that.

And in fact, when she considered it now, Rachel hoped to hell she *hadn't* known. If she had, how would she ever be able to forgive herself, for . . .

For this? For . . . abandoning Zoe. For letting her daughter be taken—no, for actually *pushing* her away.

There was simply no other way to put it. She'd led them into this. She'd *insisted* that they continue to progress along a course she *knew* was wrong; had been just as determined as Ray had been not to let anything alter their route—or even to notice anything was wrong until it was far too late.

It hadn't been a big dog, Ray insisted later. Just one of the scrawny island dogs they often saw scrounging for scraps outside Josie's or down by the wharf. But it had been fierce.

When it lunged, Rachel had still been on the line. She'd heard a strangled cry, then a loud crash as Ray dropped the phone. There were barks and yells; there was Zoe's scream and the intermittent cries of nearby kids and passersby; there were grunts and muffled shouts as Ray threw himself on the dog, kicked at it—bit, even.

He'd gone nearly out of his mind, he told Rachel later, and couldn't clearly remember the progression of events. At some point, though, he must have grabbed a stone from the street, because he remembered bringing it down as hard as he could on the dog's skull. The dog had growled and writhed, but had kept its jaw clenched firmly around Zoe's small hand.

Ray tried again, then a third time. The dog snarled and leapt, releasing Zoe's hand. It bared its teeth at Ray—its eyes blank and hard.

He must have closed his eyes then, he said, in preparation for a blow that never came. When he opened them again he saw that the dog was already halfway across the square.

Several minutes passed after that before Ray remembered Rachel on the other end of the line.

Her voice had sounded very small. Like the voice of a mouse, Zoe offered later, shouting up from a hole in the ground. "Ray! Ray! Talk to me! Ray!" Rachel had screamed. "What the hell is happening!? What the hell is going on?"

The bite had been deep but clean. They took Zoe to the clinic and the wound was scrubbed and bandaged. She was given a series of shots.

"It was an accident," Ray assured both Rachel and Zoe as they headed home. "The dog was just acting on instinct. He didn't know what he was doing. We can't blame the dog."

"But what about the feeling you had?" Rachel had pressed him later. "You said you felt uneasy. There must have been some reason for that, right? And the kids . . . When you said they were *huddled* at the fountain. Where was the dog then? What do you think they were doing?"

"Rachel," Ray had said, then paused. Sighed. "I honestly don't know what to tell you. I don't know what to say. Yes, sure —I had a feeling, but I have lots of *feelings*, don't I? So do you. Isn't it more logical—as you say—to stick to what we *know*?" He looked at her reprovingly. "It was an accident," he repeated. "And you can't blame the dog."

Rachel felt—as she had so often that fall—backed into a corner. She let the subject drop. Now, though—sitting on the floor of her office across from this kid with the gun—she cursed herself. It hadn't been just a "feeling." The threat to Zoe's safety, as well as to Ray's and her own, hadn't been "all in her head," she'd *known* that much. But it was impossible that she could have known more. Or done anything different, given the circumstances, from what she did do.

Which was to wave goodbye to Ray and Zoe as they climbed the airstairs and ducked into the tiny plane that would take them safely back to the capital.

Anyway. Rachel leaned against the drawer. It was useless to think about any of this now. She'd had no other choice at the time—or she'd felt that way, which amounted to the same thing. If she'd changed her mind and made a fuss—pressed for an immediate reassignment—she'd have looked impulsive, even unstable, difficult to please. It wasn't exactly negative thinking; it was perfectly true: if they weren't careful, they'd end up in Dakar next—or Brazzaville.

Although, then again, when you thought about it (and Rachel often did), even ending up in a "reputable" place like Frankfurt or Auckland wasn't anything like a guarantee. Logically speaking, anything could happen to anybody anywhere—and at any time. Even being returned to the capital, or getting posted to Frankfurt, could in no way protect a person from ordinary dangers quite impossible to foresee.

Rachel yanked angrily against the drawer, but it was already extended as far as it would go. The metal cuffs cut sharply into her skin.

"All right?" The kid was watching her curiously, head cocked, pen poised above his ten-cent pad. Cool. Casual. Rachel thought: He has no fucking idea what's coming to him.

But then again, neither did anyone. Neither did she.

Stay calm, she instructed herself.

The kid continued to watch her, one of his legs propped up on a knee. There was an impassiveness in the kid's stare that Rachel recognized. She'd noticed it before among the island men, and it had always disturbed her. It was like being looked at from under a rock.

The thought made Rachel feel instantly guilty. But she couldn't help it. That dull expression, the blank, glazed stare. She couldn't help but feel that there was—though surely not an inherent, inherited—at least a "cultural" stupidity to the island people. Something about growing up there in such isolation, and without any sense of the ultimate connectivity she'd always been able at some level to take for granted, that resulted in a certain irremediable stubbornness of spirit and intellect—a general lack of curiosity and ambition.

There was something almost—Rachel shuddered even to think it, but there it was—*inhuman* about the way the kid was looking at her now. She shrugged the idea from her mind. She didn't actually believe it, of course. And she could hardly be blamed, could she? Given the circumstances. For whatever unfair thoughts were occurring to her now . . .

"So you telephoned the capital," the kid was saying, twirling his pen in the air and smoothing his notebook on his propped-up knee. "Good. Fine. We telephoned them, too—a couple of hours ago. I'm sure it's a bit of a surprise, of course—changes in plans always are. But they can't be too put out, can they?" He grinned at Rachel. "After all, it's our island!"

Here the kid looked blandly through the wide glass windows before returning his gaze thoughtfully to Rachel. "Do you know that we're sinking?" he asked. He'd read about it, he said, the way that sea levels were rising. It was a natural process. Sooner or later, the kid said, all the little volcanic islands and atolls were bound to crumble and disappear. But now that the ice caps were melting, with all the pollution from China and everywhere else, what was "natural" was happening a whole lot quicker than it otherwise would have, and even within his own lifetime, the kid said, the island might be completely submerged.

Rachel shifted uncomfortably. She was still thirsty and now she needed to pee, too—hadn't in . . . what? She didn't want to guess how many hours. She'd need to ask the kid about it. The thought disturbed her. She changed position slightly in an effort to relieve some of the pressure.

"I agree with you about the ice caps," she said in as offhand a voice as she could manage. "But if you think this sort of . . . change in plans, as it were, won't make a difference to the capital, you're wrong! Everything's—everything's connected, you know. There are a lot of people . . . invested, believe me. In various ways. It's difficult to explain . . ." She felt ridiculous, but she also felt a kind of obligation to the kid. It was difficult, yes, but it was also quite necessary for *someone* to explain a few things—set the kid straight. Perhaps (she went so far as to think, smugly) if someone had bothered to do so a bit earlier, they all could have saved themselves a whole lot of trouble.

"There's a lot of history on this island," Rachel continued in her most carefully diplomatic tone, "a lot of alliances, agreements, old ties."

"So we start again," the kid said, looking at her with the same bland expression he'd had when he'd looked out the window. "We start from zero. We do things our way this time."

Rachel shook her head. "But you just can't do that," she said. She felt impatient, then angry again—could no longer sustain her measured tone. "You can't just pretend the past doesn't exist. That all things are equal. History's taught us that—again and again!"

Involuntarily this time, Rachel yanked against the desk, then swore out loud. She felt desperate all of a sudden—as if the fate of the island, the embassy, and her own personal safety rested on the possibility of her, finally, with this kid, *getting through*. But there was no way, especially under these conditions, to properly explain it. "You just can't do it!" she repeated. "You can't start from zero! You just can't!"

"Anyway," the kid said. "I didn't come here to talk about history."

Rachel tried adjusting her position again.

"We need your help," the kid said. "And we're wasting time."

"I need—" Rachel paused. "I need to use the bathroom. I need to . . . pee."

The kid grinned. "Help us first," he said. "Then we'll help you."

"I need *to pee*," Rachel said louder.

"Maps," the kid said. "We're looking for the most up-to-date maps you have of the seafloor between here and the capital."

Rachel shook her head. "Look, I just need to take a piss," she said. "You're talking to the wrong person."

"Not according to your friend," the kid said slowly. "Not according to *Phil*."

Rachel tugged violently against the desk. The pain shot down both arms. She had the sense of the room sort of folding in on itself—of things being literally upside down. So the kid knew who she was, after all.

"I need to *piss*!" she yelled.

"It's really quite easy," the kid was saying. "Just tell us where the maps are. We'll deal with everything else ourselves."

Rachel took a deep breath. She tried to calm down. "Look," she said. "I don't know what Phil told you, but it isn't true. I don't know what you're talking about. I don't—have access—don't have any—"

"I'm *sure*," the kid interrupted, "you'd rather make it easy on yourself, wouldn't you? Rather deal with me, right? Over some of my friends."

Rachel tried to take another deep breath, but something caught in her throat.

"Or maybe you want to help us with something else," the kid said thoughtfully. "We were told you might also be able to show us some even more sensitive documents."

Rachel could smell her own fear; there was no doubt that the kid, smiling calmly at her, could smell it too.

"There's been some activity at the Ø Com station Phil claims to know nothing about." The kid's eyes—trained steadily on Rachel—gleamed. "He told us *you'd* know."

The skin on Rachel's upper thigh became suddenly warm and wet. It was a beautiful relief. "I don't know what you're talking about," she said.

"What's that?" the kid asked. "I can barely hear you. Can you speak up a little? I'm talking about some sensitive documents. Maps, as well as a few other items pertaining to some *extraordinary renditions.*"

Rachel's pant leg was beginning to cool. The piss irritated her skin. She shook her head at the kid, attempted to swallow.

"Yes, that's right, Rachel," the kid said. "*Extraordinary renditions*. To be specific, I'm talking about the abduction and retention of prisoners who haven't been given the right to a proper trial."

Again Rachel shook her head; again she attempted to swallow.

"To be even more specific, I'm talking about *torture*, Rachel," the kid said, leaning in and wagging his face in front of Rachel's own. "But don't tell me—I can already guess. You'd no idea, did you?" The kid opened his mouth. He must have swallowed the gum because it was nowhere in sight. He began to laugh loudly. "Don't tell me," he repeated, still laughing. "You'd no idea. You *didn't know*!"

NINE

The whole way back to town, bouncing along in the van, beside Kurtz, who drove, Lota couldn't stop thinking: *What if it's true?*

But then, before she could even fully register what the question meant, or why she was asking it, another occurred to her: *Even if it is, what does it matter?*

She glanced sideways. Kurtz's face was perfectly smooth. Her posture, always straight, seemed somehow even straighter. She almost seemed suspended—to float a little.

In any case, Lota thought firmly, it didn't matter what the ghost said. It wasn't the past that concerned her, or any of them, now. She looked at Kurtz and she knew this—and yet, somehow, she still didn't feel it, exactly. She wished desperately that she could feel it. The way she had, very briefly, as she'd charged into the embassy behind Verbal only a few hours before.

She closed her eyes but felt only the peeling seat leather underneath her palms; her own blood thrumming through her veins. It occurred to her that she'd done the visualization exercises all wrong from the beginning. That instead of letting herself be actually transported—like Kurtz and the rest—she'd only ever been imagining things; was therefore no closer to the future now than she'd ever been.

Or was it possible, she mused, that the future had already come and gone? That it had occurred in the brief moment just as she'd crossed the threshold of the embassy building. A sort of bursting feeling, like a gunshot: all things occurring at once.

There was nothing to do now but go through the motions. Follow Kurtz, Baby Jane. There was nothing to do but view everything as if from outside, or above. To note (as she did now) that things were proceeding, more or less, exactly as planned.

But it was as if—as if she'd been left behind. Nothing seemed to be moving anymore, either toward or away from any particular goal. How easy it was after all for everything to grind suddenly to a halt.

She saw clearly: Verbal's bewildered step back. The sudden buckle at the waist, the knee. The body's sudden confusion at the logic by which it had so far been arranged.

The van bumped to a stop.

(So, there was the possibility, still—Lota thought—of arrival.)

The van door rolled back. Baby Jane jumped out and Lota followed. She moved instinctually, without thinking. The body simply obeyed.

But what, or whom?

Kurtz moved steadily, like the figure at the prow of a ship.

(So, there was direction still . . .)

Lota felt for her gun. In the weeks and months leading up

to this day, she'd often worn it as she'd paced around her rented room—back and forth from the bed to the sink, glancing at herself in the chipped mirror. More than see it (the mirror was not large enough to reflect her whole image), she could sense the difference it made in the way she moved.

Yes, there was no doubt she was more beautiful when she was wearing the gun. She became not just another island girl, but someone else—someone from television, or out of a book. She'd paced back and forth in front of the tiny mirror and felt the way her life existed outside her, in brief refractions. How everything she did, or would do, had already been reduced to a series of disconnected gestures she could hardly consider her own.

She moved—following Baby Jane this time—toward the embassy doors. If she couldn't feel as she had this morning—as if she'd entered, or was just about to enter, the future itself—she might at least, she thought, focus on the here and now. Forget Verbal and everything else. Be just: the girl in the mirror, the girl whose life *now*, and now only, took up the whole screen.

For a moment, it worked. She felt lighter, stood straighter. For a moment—as the embassy doors opened and she stepped across its threshold for the second time that day—she felt almost suspended, as Kurtz had seemed. She seemed—yes—very nearly to *float* through the entryway, to *drift* across the short hall and up the first flight of stairs.

But it didn't last. She felt the wall of heat behind her and became aware of air as something one was expected to move through—of her own body as a thing to be moved. She'd never thought about the weight of her own body before, and now—when she did—it seemed very heavy and strange. Maybe, after all, she thought, there was no way forward—no way out. Maybe Kurtz's future was no different from anybody else's—that it ended only in the repetition of single moments, each one almost exactly like the last.

Kurtz and Baby Jane were ahead of her, still mounting the stairs. Lota merely had to follow. The pattern of sweat that had drenched Verbal's shirt earlier in the day flashed—a reverse hourglass.

What, she wondered vaguely, had they done with his body?

She continued to move forward, despite the heavy feeling in her legs and feet, the sudden resistance of the air. Her footsteps echoed loudly on the steps, behind Kurtz's and Baby Jane's.

What was past was past, she reminded herself. There was only the present—and the future—to think about now. They needed maps. And any other government documents they could find—particularly those relating to the outer station. Kurtz had gotten almost nowhere with the guards, even with Norma's help, and Hal's, but then less than an hour ago Alien had called in. The maps, he said, had been filed on the embassy's third floor: the first secretary herself had informed him.

And that was not all. A range of other materials, pointing more or less directly to the Empire's involvement in the forced rendition of illegally held prisoners, could also be found there. Due to the persistent threat of leaks and cyberattacks, the secretary had explained, the information had been kept primarily in hard copy, rather than stored electronically.

Just as Kurtz had suspected: everything they wanted was right under their noses. They only had to look.

By the time Lota reached the second-floor landing her breath was coming in gasps.

What, she wondered again, had they done with Verbal's body? Her eyes burned with the effort it took not to look back.

No, she shouldn't look, she told herself. She could only move—now—in one direction. She couldn't go back—couldn't undo anything or choose another path. Couldn't take Kurtz's advice or heed the warning she'd been given (what was it? nearly four years ago now?) as Kurtz had attempted to breeze past her in front of the school.

She could've simply gone home then, stuck her head in a book. Just as Kurtz had intuited, she'd stood a reasonable chance, then, of landing a scholarship to study overseas.

But no . . . Lota tried to shake the thought from her mind. *There was only one way.* She could only move steadily forward now.

Despite her efforts, Auntie G's voice came floating back. "You're smart. This island could use a smart girl like you."

Auntie G was treasurer of the island's chapter of Nuclear Free and Independent Futures, a group that campaigned locally and sometimes internationally for political autonomy and nuclear disarmament. For years, Auntie G, like almost every other islander, had mocked Vollman almost to his face and railed against the rest of the government. "They think they can stick a puppet like him on a string, wave him about at us once in a while, and call us decolonized?"

But so far as Lota could tell, her aunt's protests—over tea in her mother's kitchen, or in front of the National Assembly building in the main square—had yielded next to nothing. Admittedly, there'd been a couple of victories. Ten years ago, for example, the Japanese had agreed to refrain from dumping radioactive waste in nearby waters. Six years ago, the French had finally signed a treaty agreeing to forgo any missile testing within a hundred-mile range. But the progress was excruciatingly slow; Auntie G was the first to admit it.

"Impotence!" Auntie G would sneer, baring her yellowed teeth and pushing back a strand of stringy grey hair. "Bloody impotence!"

Listening to her used to make Lota actually physically ill. Her neck and head would begin to throb and she wouldn't know who she despised more in those moments: Vollman, the Empire, or Auntie G.

Even though she knew it was unfair. Even though, in truth, she was proud of her auntie, had accompanied her to more than one rally at the National Assembly, and had felt—standing beside her and holding up the homemade sign she'd made—*significant*, perhaps for the first time in her life.

Still—she couldn't help it. Every time Auntie G spat out the word "impotent," praised Jesus, and sucked on her tea, Lota would begin to ache with resentment.

The scene repeated itself all through her childhood, and all the while the only thing that changed was that Auntie G's teeth became yellower, her hair more and more streaked with grey. Lota had made at least several solemn vows that she was not going to get like that herself: bitter and old. Was not going to spend her life merely railing against a system she seemed to take actual pleasure in believing would never, and could never, change.

On the other hand, she'd always been equally suspicious of violence, and rage. She'd despised Norma, for example, whenever she'd stood up to Kurtz, yet she'd also admired her, had even been strangely attracted to her—as though to something beautiful and inevitable, a moth to a flame.

But no, rage was too easy in the end, too accessible. Its trajectory too limited and familiar.

It was better, Lota thought, to be like her mother. To simply throw up her hands. It was better to be like Marcus, her brother, who (though to the Empire he was nothing more than a tool and it might take him a lifetime to get past "petty officer") actually *did* something—rather than merely erupting with anger or waving a sign. It was better to be like Lota's best friend Violet, even, who'd surprised everyone by getting pregnant in the tenth grade and dropping out of school.

It wasn't at all unusual, of course, for an island girl either to get pregnant or to drop out of school, and if Violet had been anyone else no one would have blinked. But Violet had been smart—the smartest girl in the grade, probably in the whole school. Now she had a kid, and another on the way. It was difficult for Lota to tell if she was happy, exactly—but then again, it always had been.

At the beginning of that tenth grade year, Lota's English teacher had pasted above the blackboard the words "Better to have tried and failed than never to have tried at all" in cut-out bubble letters. All year, Lota had stared at those words and thought of Violet getting plump at home, and then of Auntie G, and she couldn't quite believe it, couldn't quite trust those words. And yet she didn't want to get pregnant, like Violet; the idea horrified her. She liked babies well enough—Violet's little boy was sweet—but beyond bouncing them on her knee for a minute or two, until they cried, she didn't really know what to do with them. Besides, except for that one time with Verbal (which had been awkward and clumsy and had happened more by accident than anything else), she'd never even properly kissed a boy.

So, she didn't want to get pregnant, and she wanted even less to simply throw up her hands like her mother, drink herself into a stupor every night like her father, or take drugs like Miles. And even if she *had* wanted to simply follow orders, joining the navy was—for a girl—quite simply out of the question.

So much for not trying. Until she'd met Kurtz, it seemed her only options were to leave the island and be quietly despised, or to grow yellow and old, like Auntie G, wondering why she never had.

Lota trained her eyes ahead. Her feet—or were they Kurtz's or Baby Jane's?—pounded ahead of her, like a heavy pulse on the stairs. A left turn; the length of half a corridor.

Kurtz stopped. They were standing in front of a large metal door. Lota studied the negative imprint of a three-digit number just above eye level, which had long since been rubbed out. Kurtz jiggled at the door's handle. Quite naturally, it was locked —but only with an ordinary deadbolt. Kurtz reached into one of the deep pockets of her cargo pants and, a moment later, had sprung the lock with a bump key; the door swung open.

The room was several degrees cooler than the rest of the building. The walls—lined with identical blue and brown packing boxes—seemed to narrow at the top, to actually close in. Each box was labelled: a series of letters (indecipherable) and a date, written in either blue or black permanent marker on each side. Lota turned in slow circles, her gaze trained on the boxes and travelling from floor to ceiling. The dates, she noticed, followed a definite pattern, with the more recent dates on top and the earlier ones stacked below.

Kurtz reached for a box at around shoulder height, labelled in blue: 11/16/1997. It was evidently heavy and she inched it out slowly, her fingers slipping off the cardboard rim. When she'd managed to coax it out so that about a third of the box's length was extended from the shelf, Baby Jane stepped in and the two of them began to lower the box to the floor. Even so, it tumbled awkwardly, hitting the floor at an angle and splitting a side.

Lota stared at its spilled contents.

Sea maps, Kurtz had said. *Extraordinary renditions.*

Lota took a step back. She looked up at the boxes that still lined the walls, at all the signs and dates that spun both backward and forward in an endless spiral. The feeling of being caught inside of, and slowly strangled by a history she did not *want* to understand began to overtake her.

History could be dangerous, Kurtz had said. It could trick you into believing in it—accepting it as inevitable.

Baby Jane kicked at the box, so that more papers spilled out, littering the floor. Reprovingly, Kurtz shook her head.

Auntie G, Lota recalled, had also been wary of history. When, five or six years ago, they'd erected a monument down by the wharf in memory of the nuclear disaster and the forced deportation of 1965, Auntie G had been incensed. "Remembering," she'd said, "is the first stage of forgetting." Then she'd written the words on a sign and carried it in front of the National Assembly for nearly a week.

"We'll start here," Kurtz said, indicating the files that had settled loosely at their feet, in scattered piles, "and work our way up."

A lump had grown in Lota's throat, at the thought of Auntie G. She'd been so intent, she realized, on not ending up like her auntie—on not uselessly beating her head against a system that she couldn't change—that she hadn't noticed how much she'd already come to resemble her. Here she was (the lump stuck; Lota blinked back a swell of hot tears), surrounded by history—its falsely divided, repetitive structure almost literally pressing in on her from every side.

A box labelled 07/07/1998 slid out easily this time when Kurtz pulled, because the adjacent box had already been removed.

Baby Jane gave a quick thumbs-up sign. Lota shut her eyes tight and swallowed, hard. A third box dropped to the floor with a dull sound, like a body being slammed against a wall.

TEN

It did not take much in the end. A twist of the wrist. Alien—leaning slightly forward in his chair—his hand placed, almost casually, on his gun.

Something gave way. She told him everything.

No, she thought, after the kid was gone. One was not, after all, in control over the course and direction of one's life. There was a limited pleasure in the discovery, however, and very soon after Rachel was left with nothing but a cold hard feeling in her gut: the sudden knowledge that she was going to die.

Several whole minutes ticked by before she realized that there must have been at least a dozen other ways of handling things. She might not have had to say anything at all, she reflected—or at least not so soon.

So the kid had pointed a gun at her. But how likely was it, really, that he would have fired?

If she'd only been able to *think*, Rachel thought, gritting her teeth. Even for a moment . . .

But she hadn't been able to think.

Well, and so what. The kid—and whoever it was he was working for—had control of the entire building. If they knew what they were looking for, it was a wonder they hadn't stumbled upon it already. In point of fact, Rachel hadn't said anything that the kid didn't already know.

Besides (Rachel clenched her fists and released them in an effort to relax), despite what Phil and the kid might think, she personally knew nothing about any of this—it was all quite beyond her. Over her head.

She'd had her suspicions, of course; knew, like anyone, that "it happened"—and also (quite naturally) where, in her particular department, the "sensitive" documents were kept. But, no—despite what Phil had said and the kid had implied—she *hadn't* known; certainly none of the specifics. How could she? It wasn't her department; it never had been. It certainly wasn't now.

So, what the hell had Phil been thinking, pointing the kid to *her*? It didn't make sense!

But then—Rachel's stomach twisted—of course it didn't.

She felt suddenly, terribly cold. How stupid could she be? Phil had probably never said a word. Rachel had just practically handed the kid a billion dollars' worth of information and who knew what else, and Phil had never even said a goddamned word!

Rachel took a deep, shaky breath and tried to exhale slowly. Okay, she thought. *Okay*—still . . . It didn't matter. Would the kid even recognize the maps if he finally found them? Rachel remembered being shown one by Phil a while back: a tangle of lines with little swirls of colour. They'd looked to her like inkblots, or Rorschach tests. And as far as the other thing went . . . it wasn't exactly illegal. That certainly didn't make it right, of course—but it made it a reality. Despite what the kid believed, you couldn't wish away reality—couldn't change the course of history simply by objecting to it!

And who was to say, in the end, Rachel reflected a little further, what was "right"? She'd learned that lesson early on in the diplomatic service: insisting that something was categorically "right" or categorically "wrong" could get you into some terribly awkward conversations. It was better to simply acknowledge that things were "complicated." That there was something of value, as well as some definite shortcomings, to every side.

Rachel wiped awkwardly at her face. Well, there was no use crying about it, she told herself sharply. It was just simply true! It wasn't just a matter of diplomacy. For better or for worse, Rachel had found that the sort of cagey, noncommittal language demanded by her job was not just a shrewd "way of speaking"; it really was the only way to approach any subject matter that was truly complex.

Rachel strained to look at her watch. Neither the short nor the long hand had appeared yet, but in any case, it couldn't be much longer now . . .

It made her almost laugh to think of the kid stumbling on the maps and taking them for Rorschach tests—or combing uselessly through her personal emails (among the information she'd given the kid was her list of passcodes). She never thought she'd feel especially grateful for the fact that the sort of work she did—even at this level—was almost entirely superficial. But it was some relief for her to be able to consider, now, how nearly impossible it would be for *anyone* to detect among her endless correspondence even a shred of actual information—let alone anything recriminating.

Then again . . . who knew? Who knew who the kid was—or who he was connected to? The whole thing had so far struck Rachel as amateurish—a farce—but her only experience with hostile takeovers and political coups had been limited to the movies. Was it possible that the kid was some sort of mercenary? That he had ties to Russia? The Middle East?

The thought unsettled her. No matter how hard she tried to push it out of her mind, it returned. The idea was wild—but it did explain a few things. It explained why, for example, she was still tied to her desk, dammit; why she was still sitting on the floor with her pants wet; why she'd just spent a brief but uncomfortable minute staring down the barrel of a gun.

But how plausible was it that a regular island kid had found his way into foreign intelligence, or transnational crime?

Rachel's mind raced. She attempted to recall the exact content of her recent email exchanges. That was the thing with intelligence, though, she reminded herself (drawing mostly from what she'd learned from TV). It wasn't necessarily about what you knew or had to hide. It was about the things you were blind to, the things you *didn't* know, or didn't *know* you knew.

Rachel thought of the kid's menacingly blank stare. Then again, in this case, she reasoned, it clearly wasn't a matter of intelligence.

Anyway—she stopped herself—it didn't matter. The thing was done. As she'd always told Ray, when his imagination got the better of him: "You've done everything you can reasonably do, haven't you? All we can do now is hope for the best."

Hope for the best!

Only now did it occur to her how ridiculous, how almost perfectly meaningless the phrase was. Only very slightly better, when you thought about it, than some of the absurd-sounding platitudes Ray's Baptist parents were fond of using. Whenever Ray had slipped up and used one himself, Rachel had amused herself by inquiring politely when she should expect him to start speaking in tongues.

She leaned toward the desk in an effort to relieve some of the pressure on her wrists and her knees. She'd simply taken it for granted, she realized, with a confused sense of resentment and shame—taken it, to a certain extent, yes, on *faith*—that her own vague reassurances were fundamentally more sincere and more rational than miracle deliverance and visions of hell. Now she wasn't so sure . . .

She began to rock a little—a rhythmic pattern that soothed her. Yes, she'd taken it for granted! Had believed, for no other reason than that she'd *wanted* to believe, that the future was bound to arrive bigger and brighter than either their present or their past. She'd *believed*—yes! Rachel thought (lurching forward a bit, then struggling to restore her balance) that the future, like the pre-crash housing market, would be boundless and unconditional; that (just as she'd written in the essay that had gained her entry, and a decent scholarship, to the Foreign Service Institute) the world was, and would continue to be, "of their own making," and that the sheer energy of her own desire could not fail to make it "a better place."

When she shifted her weight again she realized that she'd begun to lose feeling in her left leg. She flexed her foot, tried to shake it a little. The leg ached, then tingled painfully.

At best she'd been naive, she thought—at worst, dishonest. But all her life, she'd been frankly encouraged (Rachel flexed her foot again and swore softly) to expound upon empty, practically meaningless topics and themes; to use meaningless words. The smiley faces that had always graced her high school English papers reared their absurd heads suddenly—seemed to mock her. Yes, there was no other way to put it: she'd been dishonest. She'd not only grown accustomed to meaninglessness; she'd actually come to rely on it.

Even when she'd protested, there was something empty about the gesture, insincere. Something far more honest, in the end, about Ray's placid acceptance, about the way he never quite "saw the point." She'd crinkle her forehead at him across dinner tables or event halls every time her bullshit detector sounded the alarm, and he'd merely grin back—or shrug. She'd complain about evasion and abstraction, insisting that they address only what she liked to call "actual problems," and he'd answer with a brief, distracted nod.

It had been like that from the beginning—even back as far as their first date. Rachel remembered it clearly: how she'd been obliged to do most of the talking, how polite Ray had been—how anxious to please. She'd bragged a lot, she recalled. About how she'd made it through her entire undergraduate career practically without attending a single class. Instead she'd signed up for every practicum and internship opportunity she could; she'd volunteered at a rehab clinic, delivered needles out of the back of a van. All in all, it had been a far more meaningful experience, she'd told Ray proudly, than writing an essay on drug abuse statistics and trends. "The War on Drugs," she'd continued (the topic of Ray's own senior thesis), "and everything that went with it" was just lip service—didn't he know that? A conspiracy—a sham.

It was an aggressively casual place they'd chosen that night—like so many of the restaurants that had begun to spring up in the newly fashionable parts of town. It was the kind of place you took someone when you didn't want to seem as though you were trying too hard.

"They think if they just call it something it'll be that thing," Rachel had said. "But you can't declare war on something that doesn't even exist. I mean, you can't pretend it's not all part of something much bigger—that the entire system doesn't have to change!"

They were both drinking red wine out of Mason jars and, after only a glass and a half, Rachel could feel that her face had flushed and she was aware that, at best, Ray was only half listening. Then Ray had reached abruptly across the table and placed his hand on Rachel's cheek. She stopped speaking and stiffened, but Ray did not pull back. He was looking at her intently—almost too intently. His eyes seemed to go right through her. He brushed his thumb against her lower lip. Rachel slapped him; he reeled back.

"Why did you do that?"

Ray said nothing. His hand was still semi-extended, hovering emptily over his plate.

"Men always think they can *do* that," Rachel said, her throat tightening a little and feeling, for some inexplicable reason, like she wanted to cry. It took a few moments before she could trust herself to look up. When she did, she could tell that Ray was genuinely perplexed, that he regretted his action, tremendously—but didn't know why.

"Do . . . what?" he asked finally.

"I was *talking*!"

Ray blinked. "Oh," he said. "Oh. Right. I'm sorry."

Rachel felt herself relax. She took a sip of wine, then set the jar down carefully on the table, examining the way the wine collected along the spiralled rim. "Not everything a woman says," she warned him (she could feel his eyes on her still—really *looking at her*—but she did not yet look up), "is for the purposes of getting into bed."

But later on, of course, they did end up in bed. Just as—in that moment—he and she both knew they would.

A muffled sound from a nearby office startled Rachel. A shout, or a sob, perhaps—almost certainly human. She tried to guess what direction it had come from, but she'd become strangely disoriented and had trouble placing it.

Should she respond in some way? Slam against the desk, or stomp on the floor? Shout?

She pictured the ambassador. She pictured Bradley, next door. Downstairs there was Monique, the administrative assistant—a gregarious, extremely flirtatious woman in her late fifties who always seemed to be gasping for air. Had they also had their hands bound? Had a gun waved in their faces? And if so (Rachel shifted her weight uncomfortably), had they also crumbled—under only the slightest of pressures? Had they . . . wet themselves? Cried? Handed over their passwords?

To be fair—Rachel reminded herself—having a gun waved in one's face was not exactly the "slightest of pressures." And in her case, handing over "everything" was, practically speaking, very nearly the same as handing over nothing at all.

But then she thought of the ambassador again, and of the new intern, Fiona—a viciously thin woman with almost translucent skin. It was really impossible to know how ordinary people would act given extraordinary circumstances. She wasn't proud, necessarily, of the way she'd behaved, but she really couldn't blame herself either. All things considered, she decided, she'd done fairly well in remaining as optimistic as she had—in keeping things in perspective, in remembering that, despite appearances, the power remained almost wholly on her side. Still, it irked her how quickly all of that had dissolved the moment the kid had threatened her, touched his gun.

There was the sound again; Rachel strained to listen. She could hear almost nothing, however, over the insistent throbbing of her own pulse.

She tried to breathe. In. In. Out. In. In. Tried to look at the situation from a different perspective—from some distant point in the future, or the past. Tried to see the way that what was happening to her was connected to everything else in her life . . . Yes, she would get through this, she told herself. Years, months, or even weeks later, she would look back on this moment and it would be almost as if it had happened to somebody else.

There it was—the sound again. Like a voice being stuffed back in a throat. A moan, a muffled shout—

Before she could stop herself, Rachel's own voice rang out. The noise almost choked her.

Stupid!

She could feel the blood beating in her ears and under her tongue. The kid would come running now, almost certainly. Bring his friends—wave his gun.

A minute or more passed and nothing happened. Rachel held her breath until she almost passed out, and listened, but no sound came.

ELEVEN

Mr. Joshua stood watch at the gated entry to the enclave of newer homes, built on a small rise just north of the town centre, which housed the island's foreign residents. Though not particularly luxurious by anything but island standards, the houses —with their fresh paint, big windows, and landscaped front yards—looked enormous and out of place to anyone who, like Mr. Joshua, had travelled up the hill from town.

Lota nodded to Mr. Joshua as they sped through the gate. She felt calm now—almost like herself again: the girl who'd dressed in front of the chipped mirror that morning, who'd felt the future taking shape inside her before anything had even begun.

It hadn't taken them long, back at the embassy, to find what they were looking for. The boxes stacked on the middle shelves were stuffed with memos and intelligence reports dating back to the early 1990s. At the very top of the pile they'd found maps, scientific reports, and a detailed record of depth measurements between here and the two coasts. Kurtz had been pleased, to say the least, and it began to feel obvious even to Lota that—despite their mistakes—they were moving steadily toward their goal.

The van stopped in front of a pink ranch house with a painted iron gate. Baby Jane jumped out and Lota jumped out after. She felt the gravel crunch beneath her feet as she trailed Kurtz through the busted front door into the house.

Inside, everything was neat and bare, as if nobody had ever actually lived in the house. Lota had the eerie feeling that, if she continued toward the back, she'd find that the rear rooms gaped—that there would be no facing wall.

They crossed the soft linoleum floor, Kurtz's boots squishing noisily. But then the hall ended and the linoleum gave way to thick carpet. When Kurtz stepped onto the carpet and raised her gun, her boots made absolutely no sound.

Lota was standing directly behind Kurtz and, from that position, couldn't see what Kurtz was pointing her gun at. Because of this, she didn't know where exactly—or at what—she should be pointing her own.

She could have taken a step to either side, of course; there was nothing stopping her. But she just stood there instead—her pulse beating powerfully, biting at her top lip until the skin broke.

Very slowly, Kurtz edged her way forward and, reluctantly, Lota raised her gun. She didn't budge, though, and it was a good several seconds even after Kurtz had sufficiently moved ahead before she realized what it was she was looking at, and at whom she was pointing her gun.

It was a woman.

Lota's hands began to tremble.

And a child.

Lota looked at Kurtz, but Kurtz was looking only steadily ahead. The woman—clearly unarmed—stared back, gripping her son. Her eyes were bloodshot and her short thin hair practically stood up on end.

"Put the child down." Kurtz's voice sounded distressingly calm.

The woman retracted an outstretched arm; Lota lowered her gun. The child—a boy of three, perhaps, four at most—began to wail.

"I said, *put the child down*."

The woman shook her head. Her face was pale—red in patches. She didn't speak; possibly she couldn't.

Lota stepped forward. It was not a decision she made but instead almost an involuntary response. Before she could stop herself she had taken a step and reached out one hand in the direction of the child.

"Here," she said. "Here. Let me . . ." She took another step and placed her other hand firmly on the muzzle of Kurtz's gun.

Again the woman shook her head, but a moment later, when Lota stretched both of her hands toward the child, the woman released him.

Abruptly, the child stopped crying. He looked first at Lota and then back at his mother, clinging tightly all the while to Lota's shoulder and the collar of her shirt.

"*Get down*." Kurtz's voice was strained now, in a way that Lota didn't recognize.

The woman dropped heavily to her knees; Baby Jane swooped in. She took a piece of rope from her belt and swiftly tied the woman's hands. The child watched, still clinging to Lota's shirt. She could feel the way his body trusted hers—instinctively. He did not cry out.

"We're not here to hurt you." Kurtz's voice was steady again, but at the sound of it the woman began to bawl loudly.

"Quiet!" A shrill, reflexive response, which Kurtz could not have intended. "We'll be transferring you to town. You—*and* your son—will be well looked after."

Baby Jane hoisted the woman up and thrust her forward, in the direction they'd come. Lota followed with the child.

"We'll keep you in our custody," Kurtz continued, taking up the rear, "only until further arrangements can be made."

They went out the front door, then down the steps to the drive. The woman's body had gone limp; Baby Jane struggled to lift her. Finally, with Kurtz's help, she managed to slide her into the narrow back seat of the van. Lota set the child down beside her. The woman couldn't hold him properly, but her body curved around him. As it did so, the boy gave out a single, jagged sob.

Lota moved to the front passenger-side door and was just about to squeeze, next to Baby Jane, inside, when Kurtz stopped her; grabbed her by the wrist. "What do you think you're doing?" she hissed. "How dare you put your hands on my gun?"

Lota could feel Kurtz's hot breath, the shape of the words on her skin. She looked up, surprised by the unexpected intimacy and directness of the address. She'd never been that close to Kurtz, had never seen her face like this—been able to examine its wrinkles and pores. She'd never been able to stare so long, or so frankly, into the older woman's eyes, which appeared as distant stars; somehow, at the same time, very close and very far away.

"Do you hear me?"

Lota said nothing. She couldn't tell what difference it would make if she responded or did not, so she simply stared back, mesmerized.

Kurtz gave Lota's wrist another violent tug. "Watch out," she said. "You remember who gives the orders around here." Her eyes flashed. In, out. Far, near. It was impossible to understand where the light was coming from—or how far away it was.

They moved quickly through the other houses. The van filled. Some of the foreigners cried, like the woman from the first house. Some were angry and threatened them, but most complied easily—were almost deferential. They appeared bewildered, uncertain why things were not following their expected course and anxious to do whatever they could to get things back on track again.

Almost all of them had soiled themselves. When Lota got out in the parking lot of the school gymnasium and opened the van door, the smell hit her like a wall. The sun was still high at that time, but the heat had changed—become heavy. It would probably rain soon. Lota tried to catch the eye of the little boy as they led the prisoners through the gymnasium doors but could not. He was clinging to his mother and did not look up.

Dazed, Lota walked back to the van. She found Bruno there, his large body hunched, talking on his cell. Kurtz was still in the front passenger seat; Norma, Mystique, and Alien were sprawled out in back. Lota climbed in. Then Baby Jane, Killmonger, and Hannibal Lecter arrived. Bruno revved the motor. He still had the phone tucked under his double chin, though he didn't any longer appear to be talking to anyone.

Beside him, Kurtz sat up terrifically erect. As they drove back toward the centre of town, she seemed to physically *hum*.

The clock tower and then the Birdman came into view.

Kurtz glanced back and—briefly—her eyes caught Lota's. Lota felt the pressure of her gaze and the white ghost's words came swimming back. "A bit of a psycho . . . Everybody knew."

Bruno hit the pedal and the van lurched forward. Lota did her best to push the words aside.

"Yes," Kurtz said. She'd turned around again and was tapping the dash. "Yes, yes, yes."

Lota's stomach twisted. She leaned across Alien, toward the window. She desperately needed air.

Surely the white ghost had been lying, she thought. Or confused. Surely he'd been thinking about someone else. He'd referred to Kurtz as Santos—probably the most common surname on the island. He could've been talking about practically anyone.

"All right?" Alien said, shifting slightly. Gratefully, Lota lunged toward the window. The air felt like water on her skin. But the doubt would not leave her.

What, after all, she wondered as she stared out the window and inhaled great gulps of warm air, did she really know about Kurtz? Everything she'd told them about herself—as well as everything she'd taught them about both the future and the past—had been based on a willing embrace of a series of fictions. She'd constructed her entire army out of stories—out of lies!

The sun had just begun to lick at the water, to touch the tops of the waves. There were no clouds in that part of the sky and it looked as though the sun had been cut out of paper or cloth. Lota gripped the plastic cover of the seatback in front of her and leaned away from the window. Soon, she thought, the sun would begin to set slowly. It would billow slightly at the bottom as it hit the water, then quickly sink from view. Ordinarily, Lota loved to watch it go—loved to glimpse, if she could, the strange green flash across the surface of the water in the exact moment the sun disappeared below the waves—to feel the strange vertigo induced by forcing herself to think, as she often did, *It is not the sun slipping, incrementally, away from me; it is me slipping incrementally away from the sun.*

But today she closed her eyes; she couldn't look.

"Yes," Kurtz said again, drumming on the dash. "Yes, yes, yes." She sat erect. Not just her body but the very air around her seemed to hum.

The evening had begun to cool slightly. The breeze had picked up, and now—thankfully—it began to blow itself in through the van's semi-open windows.

Well, what was there, in the end, but stories? Lota thought. Lies? And what was any revolution, as Kurtz had said and Norma, it seemed, had always implicitly known, but *necessary violence*? A total break—"as though by an unbridgeable chasm" —with the past?

Even if it *was* true, what the ghost had said . . .

The earth had been formed by a collision of opposing elements. Romulus slew Remus, Cain slew Abel, Pele was the goddess of volcanoes and fire as well as the creator of islands, and the origin of all life: "whatever brotherhood human beings may be capable of has grown out of fratricide, whatever political organization men may have achieved has its origin in crime."

Lota gripped the seatback tighter. Yes, she thought. What was any revolution, therefore, but this? Yes, *this*. Despite her personal doubts and misgivings. The revolution—the future—was *this*. Was Kurtz drumming her hand on the dash. Was the sound of her voice as it beat out the time. Was—

Yes! This island. This air. Was *yes* this water. This dirt, this van, this rutted road.

It was a relief to breathe again. A moment ago Lota had been practically suffocating, but now, she realized, there was plenty of air. She inhaled deeply, but just as she was about to exhale, the breath snagged in her throat.

She saw Verbal. His eyes glazed over in the moment after the shot—before his body or mind even knew what had hit him.

Lota gagged, choking on spit and air.

Alien shifted beside her. "All right?" he said again.

Yes, it was Verbal's eyes that had given in first. She'd glimpsed in them—even before the waist and then the knees buckled—what? A profound relief. Yes, that was it. The same relief she'd felt just a moment ago as she (*Yes!*) had given in, too, allowing—no, inviting—the past to simply slip away.

She hadn't suspected it. No. Until that moment, couldn't possibly have guessed that the future into which she'd wished, so desperately, to arrive was the same future into which—

Again she saw Verbal. He rose up, an apparition on the road. Bruno did not slow down. The van bounced, careering forward. Verbal stared, his eyes turned inward. They refused to look, refused to see the van approaching—were as powerless as Lota was to steer the vehicle in any other direction than the one in which it was already bound.

But then, just as rapidly as it had appeared, the vision faded. There was nothing but the road, the Birdman up ahead. Graffitied and shat upon by generations of rock doves and common terns. Verbal was safe—was untouched, unmoved. At the last minute—just before the van hit—his eyes must have shifted, just as they had earlier that day. He'd plunged inward, escaping contact—intent on something beyond her, which she couldn't understand.

They'd almost reached the main avenue now; Bruno slowed the van to a crawl. Kurtz leaned out the window, a megaphone gripped in one hand. Even the air seemed to hold its breath.

Then the sun hit the water and Kurtz let out a loud, long yell. The sound boomed through the megaphone and echoed out onto the empty street.

For the first time, it occurred to Lota how odd it was to see the streets so deserted. Usually, at this time of day, people had begun to creep out of their houses again, to sit on their front steps, or the benches outside Josie's canteen, to smoke and tell stories, or simply to sit in silence and watch the sun go down.

But no one was out on their front steps today. No old-timers sat nodding on the benches outside Josie's—as though in agreement with something no one had actually heard. No kids threw balls against the wall of the credit union building or chased each other around the broken fountain or the National Assembly's concrete steps.

Only Kurtz's voice could be heard. As though it was just a voice—disconnected even from the idea of human beings.

It was impossible to say how long the yell lasted. Although it seemed like hours, even days, from the time it began to the time that it ended, the van travelled only a few hundred feet: from where the parking lot next to the National Assembly building emptied out onto the main road to the big shade tree outside Josie's canteen.

At some point during that stretch—of distance or of time—and without Lota's having witnessed it, the sun had disappeared below the line of the horizon. The streets had immediately been plunged into shadow.

Just as Lota was noticing this, Kurtz lifted the megaphone again and began to speak into the descending darkness. She spoke slowly this time, in discrete syllables, but somehow this did not make the voice seem any more human—or what she said any easier to understand.

"For-ty-three years of des-pot-ism and corruption," the voice said. "Of put-ting for-eign int-er-ests a-head of our own." It was as if the voice wished to communicate the syllables themselves—and not the words, or their possible meanings. "This time is now at an end. A new e-ra is born."

The syllables bounced down the empty street, then disappeared, splintering through the leaves of the lead trees.

Norma, clutching a second megaphone and leaning out a rear window, repeated the words. Then she handed the megaphone to Mr. Joshua, beside her, who repeated the words a third time.

Still, no life stirred in the streets. No one emerged from the houses. No one made their way to the Assembly steps or pulled up a chair outside Josie's canteen or stood gaping at them from the side of the road.

"We can as-sure you," Kurtz called out. "Voll-man and his fam-il-y are quite safe. I re-peat: their safety and se-cur-it-y—like your own—is guar-an-teed."

Perhaps everyone, Lota mused, had followed the sun to the edge of the water—had walked out to that limit, then past it, been suddenly drowned. Or perhaps no one had ever lived on the island at all. Perhaps Lota had dreamed it all up, and Kurtz was announcing the liberation of an island that had never existed, a people that had never been born.

Kurtz's voice again. "We pro-mise to ensure," she said, "that basic hu-man rights and freedoms will be recog-nized. That law and order will be rein-stat-ed. That democra-cy will pre*vail*!"

The syllables came close, this time, to making an actual impression on the air. Norma repeated them, then Mr. Joshua.

Then Kurtz again. "Re-joice."

Just as before, the word sounded at first only like two distinct syllables, but then Kurtz repeated it. "Re-joice," she said. "Let the is-land re-joice"—until slowly, the syllables became words, and the words took on meaning.

As they did so, the people began to emerge. Singly, at first. Then in groups of three or four. They stood out in their small yards—stared wide-eyed as though at the wreckage after a storm.

But nothing had been ruined. No leaf had been shaken—no stone dislodged or overturned. Except for the brief wind that had blown in from the water just before the sun went down, the air had hardly stirred all day. No, there was nothing at all to indicate that anything had changed. People stood on their doorsteps, on the side of the road, in the middle of the street, and looked around and were surprised because everything was different, and yet nothing had changed. They looked at the dirt on the street, at the broken fountain, the concrete steps, the leaning branches of the lead trees.

"Re-joice!" the voice rang.

The islanders stumbled from their homes. They gazed around and saw—briefly, and all together—that everything that existed in that moment existed only as it had always existed.

"Rejoice!"

They saw that even what hadn't yet happened, or wasn't yet real, would exist like that, too: as it already was.

But then something shifted. Instead of one shared feeling, there were many. People began to see the world and what was happening in it as they had before: from their own distinct, and limited, and therefore often conflicting angles. As this happened, the looks on people's faces turned variously to anger, confusion, excitement, or disbelief.

An old woman stood at the side of the road, carrying a chicken. Lota looked at the woman and the woman looked steadily back. It was Lota's turn to feel angry, and then—almost immediately—ashamed. At the woman's absolutely unreadable expression, which Lota recognized as her own. At the way the old woman just *stood there*, clutching a chicken under one arm. As though she did not—as Lota herself in that moment did not—understand the meaning of simple words.

TWELVE

Rachel began to hear shouts in the distance—once in a while the gunning and popping of a motor outside. Inside, everything was quiet. She began to wonder if she'd been forgotten, left entirely alone.

But then, that was impossible. There was the ambassador; there was Bradley next door; there was Jason, the accountant; Fiona, Monique . . .

She shut her eyes firmly and thought back to her ordinary breakfast that morning, to her conversation with Grigor in the car. A few hours ago, all of this—the hard floor, the handcuffs, the settling dusk outside—had been as distant and unimaginable as that ordinary breakfast seemed to her now. A few hours ago, her only concern had been that Ray had not yet returned her call. The thought caused a brief but severe spasm of pain in her lower abdomen. If only—she thought urgently, for the thousandth time—she'd negotiated, scheduled an earlier return. Even by just a few days; that's all it would have taken! If only she'd left in November (Rachel's palms had begun to sweat), or better yet had never set foot on the island at all.

She'd suggested it. A day or two after the offer came through, and in all earnestness. It bothered her, she'd said to Ray, to see the way that it evidently bothered *him* that she'd been promoted and he had not. Because he was absolutely right. It really *wasn't* fair, and perhaps it would be better for both of them if—

"I never said it bothered me," Ray had snapped.

"Not in so many words . . ."

Ray squinted at her. "Why are you doing this?"

Rachel did not want her response to Ray's question to come back to her now; did not want to recall how quickly and apologetically she'd agreed with Ray. She was making a fuss over nothing. Despite her genuine misgivings, she and he both knew that she was going to take the job. That she was "delighted" to take it (the exact word she'd chosen in her brief email to the ambassador), and both pleased and proud that she'd been selected for the position ahead of Ray.

Rachel concentrated on the steady thrum of her heart in her chest, the insistence with which her blood continued to course through her veins.

It was stupid to think this way; stupid to remember things. Or to feel ashamed when you didn't even know of what exactly, and, anyway, couldn't change or undo anything.

She heard Ray's voice again. It echoed accusingly in her brain: "Why are you doing this?"

Her eyes filled with tears.

All day, she realized, she'd kept expecting to wake up—to half chuckle to herself about the way that the ordinary elements of her everyday life had combined to create such a ridiculous dream. But it had now been—what? Twelve hours or more since she'd telephoned the capital. Twelve hours or more since they'd known that something on the island was terribly wrong . . .

Then a thought struck. She felt her throat close. How had the idea not occurred to her before? It was not, and never had been, she realized, the *island* that was important to the Empire. What was important was that the island *did not actually exist*.

For the first time, it all seemed to Rachel appallingly clear. She thought of Alien. How cocky the kid had been, how ignorant and self-assured. Well, however ignorant he'd been, she'd been more ignorant still! How, she wondered, rubbing roughly at her scalp and forehead with her shackled hands, had it not occurred to her before? How had she not *known*?

The world would soon be run from a single island, the Empire's chief security officer had said. But what he'd meant was that the world would soon be run from *no place at all*. What he'd meant was that the government, like the global economy, had become literally utopian—had gone clean off the map.

Rachel shivered. The air conditioning had been left on; her sweat and piss were cold on her skin. If the Empire was planning to, or already was, running the entire planet from an island that didn't actually exist, well—Rachel thought, still rubbing at her head and neck and hugging her knees to her chin—the Empire didn't exist. Perhaps it had never existed!

Yes, perhaps, Rachel considered (she was even becoming strangely excited by the thought), to recognize any form of government was for that form to have already begun to break down. Perhaps that's what a state was, she thought feverishly, all it had ever been: the after-effect of a force that had already been exerted, and did not, now, properly exist at all.

She recalled, for some reason, how, shortly before her father had died in bed of lung cancer at the age of sixty-five, he'd raised himself up with a strength he hadn't had for months or even years and tried to stumble his way to the door. He'd seemed confused—as though he didn't know who or where he was, or who his family was, or why, for some horrifying reason, they seemed so intent on keeping him down.

Afterward, Rachel learned that sudden bursts of energy were not uncommon leading up to the moment of death. Something about sensory neurons, the central nervous system. But this did little to assuage the guilt Rachel continued to feel over the fact that—despite her uneasy sense in that moment that there must be some alternative—it had been she herself who'd forced her father back to his bed.

An hour later her father was gone. His breath had caught suddenly—he'd choked a little, but just as if he'd swallowed wrong. Then that was it. His eyes went blank and his skin grey.

Rachel had not been raised with any particular religion and, she realized now—in lieu of the colourful, frankly terrifying images Ray had always had in his head of the resurrection and the last judgment—she'd always pictured the end of the world looking more or less like her father had looked a moment or so after he died. The light just going, suddenly, out. The world appearing not as itself, but as a pale imitation of something else —a dull monument to a brief, ruined fantasy.

So the island didn't exist! All along, it had been little more than a symbol, a metaphor—in itself just as dispensable as everything else. The system had, Rachel thought (she was feeling almost triumphant now), been entirely diffused, the end goal of every political structure already achieved.

A car door banged and footsteps clattered up the walk. Every hair on Rachel's body stood up suddenly on end.

The footsteps grew louder; there was a sound like the front door being opened. Rachel's heart pounded, the footsteps hammered up the stairs. They were—she realized—very definitely now headed in her direction, perhaps even directly to her door.

The moment she realized it, her heart stopped beating entirely.

Then the door burst open, a woman entered, and Rachel's pulse returned in a powerful surge.

She was of medium height, with freckled brown skin and a shock of curly grey hair. She moved quickly, her head high, her eyes pointed straight ahead, and, at first, seemed either not to notice, or not to care, that there was anyone else in the room. But then she turned and—her heavy boots planted at least two feet apart—stood facing Rachel squarely.

A moment later, an enormously fat man—wearing an oversized dress shirt stained under the armpits and army fatigue trousers—and the kid, Alien, pushed in behind. They stood together, crowded at the entrance, the kid's eyes twitching from side to side—a bored rather than a nervous motion.

"Good evening."

The woman's voice was cool, smooth, vaguely apologetic. "We wanted to thank you," she said, "to thank you *sincerely* for your support so far. I don't know if it's been made clear to you exactly . . . what it's meant."

Rachel felt a bubble of panic rising in her throat.

"You are, I hope," the woman continued—the expression on her face was absolutely unreadable—"still willing to help?"

Rachel cleared her throat and shifted her weight to release some of the pressure from her wrists. The woman stood facing her, arms folded firmly across her chest.

"I suppose," Rachel said finally, in a weak voice she instantly resented, "it would depend . . ."

"Of course," the woman said. Her eyes softened slightly. "I can appreciate that."

The fat man stepped forward. "We'd like you to deliver a message," he said. "To the capital. Directly to the head of state."

Rachel said nothing.

The fat man took another step forward, squatted, and began fumbling at the lock on Rachel's wrists.

The lock sprang; the woman smiled.

Rachel was vaguely aware of her wet trousers—of the possible piss smell she gave off—but she didn't have time to dwell on this long. The fat man had already grabbed her under each arm and now hoisted her up roughly so that she was forced to stand. She felt light-headed. For a moment, her vision blackened at the corners. She thought she might pass out.

Still smiling, the woman picked up the phone from the floor. She slid it across the desk, then handed Rachel a flipped-open spiral-bound notebook and pointed with her index finger to the top of the page. The message was excessively legible, written in oversized block letters, but still, Rachel had difficulty reading it. Her eyes kept skimming over the contents; the letters blurred and wobbled strangely on the page. She could feel the woman's eyes on her, could feel the way she wasn't smiling anymore.

"Read it."

Rachel blinked.

"*Read it.*"

Rachel cleared her throat. "'When,'" she began unsteadily—but then her voice failed. She forced herself to breathe. "'When,'" she began again, "'in the course of human events . . .'"

She blinked twice. Looked up. The woman was smiling again. A cold shiver ran up and down Rachel's spine.

"*Read it.*"

"'. . . it becomes necessary for one people,'" Rachel continued. Her vision clouded. Her brain felt exceedingly slow. "'For one people,'" she continued, "'to dissolve the political' . . . But wait, hold on a minute." Rachel looked up. She was pretty sure the woman was still smiling, but her vision had blackened at the corners again and she could barely make her out.

"Please," the woman urged. "Keep going—please."

Rachel looked down at the notebook, more or less because she needed something to focus on. Her vision cleared slightly.

"'To dissolve the political bands which have connected them' . . ." Her eyes skipped ahead. No, she was not mistaken.

What the hell? What was this? Some kind of practical joke? But no. There was something sinister in it, too. In the absurdity of it all.

The woman had stopped smiling. She was just standing there now, looking at Rachel—feet planted squarely, arms folded—no expression on her face. Rachel felt ashamed suddenly and glanced away. But then—ashamed of herself for feeling ashamed—she glanced back again. The woman's eyes were still on her. Rachel glanced away; it seemed impossible to hold the woman's gaze. And yet . . . the more she looked the more she wanted to look. There was something fascinating about the woman—irresistible, almost. She couldn't understand it.

Again the woman smiled. "Please," she said gently, nodding toward the page. "Continue . . . Please."

Obediently, Rachel bent over the notebook. "'We hold these truths to be self-evident,'" she read, though she was pretty sure she'd skipped a bit, "'that all men and women are created equal, that they are endowed by their Creator with certain unalienable Rights—'" It was too much; she couldn't bear it.

The woman was still smiling.

"I don't," Rachel said weakly. "I don't understand. You want me to . . . to read this? To . . . the president?"

The fat man had moved to the window. The kid was shifting from one foot to the next.

Still smiling, the woman leaned across Rachel's desk and picked up the phone. She tapped a number in swiftly, then double-checked it on the screen. A half-second later the sound of a phone ringing on the other side of the world echoed loudly. The woman stepped back. The phone rang again. Rachel wondered—almost disinterestedly—what would happen when someone picked up.

She would scream, she thought. As soon as she heard a voice on the other end, she would open her mouth and she would scream. That at least would alert whoever was on the other end that something on the island was terribly wrong.

But her throat felt painfully dry, and (there was no use denying it) she was morbidly afraid. She worried, because of this, that despite her conviction, if someone did pick up she'd be unable to make a sound.

What didn't occur to her was that she'd simply do as she was told; the possibility didn't even enter her mind.

But that was exactly what she did. After four rings, the line clicked.

"State Department, hello. How may I direct your call?"

The fat man was hovering beside her, breathing heavily. Rachel could almost taste the impression his sour breath made on her skin.

"I—I'd like to speak to the president," Rachel said. Her tone was tentative, apologetic—but there could be no mistake as to what had been said. Her voice had been level and clear, the words plainly intelligible.

Nonetheless, there was a confused sound on the other end, then a number of clicks. Rachel feared she'd been cut off. Despite her horror at what was happening, the thought filled her with sudden dread. All at once, she didn't care what she had to say to the president, or anyone else—just as long as the connection was not broken, just as long as she could be certain that someone remained there, on the other end of the line.

"Hello?" she said, her voice rising wildly. "Is anyone there? Hello?"

"Yes," another voice said. "Can I have your name, please?"

"Rachel Darling."

There was another low rustling sound. "Hello, Ms. Darling," the voice replied. "I'm transferring you directly to the president. Hold just a moment, please."

Then, unbelievably, there was the president—his voice sounding just as it did in the television debates. Casual, possibly a little bored, as though Rachel was in the habit of making distress calls to the Department of State.

"Hello, this is the president speaking."

"I've been asked to deliver a message," Rachel said hurriedly. "Shall I . . . shall I read it to you now?"

The question was directed not to the voice on the other end of the line but rather to the woman beside her. She couldn't help it; she turned slightly.

What was she looking for?

The woman stepped closer. She stood so close now that Rachel could see the tiny veins that studded the edge of her high forehead.

"Yes, go ahead," the president's voice said.

Rachel stared at the pattern of veins on the woman's forehead, felt the fat man's sour breath on her skin.

She inhaled deeply. "'*When,*'" she began, "'in the course of human events . . .'"

She'd only got about halfway through when the telephone clicked again and another voice interrupted. "Ms. Darling, Ms. Darling. *Ma'am.* There seems to be some mistake. Ms. Darling?"

The veins on the woman's forehead darkened—stood out more urgently under her skin.

"Keep going," she said.

Rachel continued. Quickly now—stumbling over the words. The woman's lips began to curl. The line cracked. Once or twice a voice interrupted: "Ms. Darling? Is that you? Excuse me, Ms. Darling?" But she kept reading until the end and finished dazed —nearly panting for breath.

THIRTEEN

Mad Max had parked a flatbed police truck next to Josie's canteen and was busy unloading kegs of confiscated liquor. Gradually at first, and then more steadily, the islanders drifted toward the square. They stood together in little groups, interrupting each other, repeating themselves. When they could no longer hear one another over the growing din, they shouted, gesticulating wildly with their hands.

Then the music started and there was nothing but Mannie Groening's trumpet and the heat rising from the cracked pavement. Lani Harris was on guitar. After a while, Greg Nugent picked up his three-stringed uke.

By the time Lota arrived, the liquor had been flowing for nearly an hour. The shouting had given way to dancing, the dancing to a frenzied, directionless movement, to which there seemed neither origin nor end.

But then, abruptly, the music stopped. Mad Max had clambered onto the flatbed wearing his police uniform. At first, when the islanders turned to look at him, they didn't know for certain what side he was on, or for that matter what side they were on—but then he pumped his fist into the air, and it didn't matter anymore.

"*History begins now!*" he shouted. Mannie Groening put his trumpet to his lips and blew. "Will you *free yourselves*?" Mad Max raised his arms above his head, palms outward so that they stretched toward the crowd. "Will you *defend* your rights as *patriots* and *human beings*?"

There was a rousing cheer; Mannie Groening's trumpet blared. Then Lin Ainsley started in on some homemade drums and the people began to tremble and sway to the beat. Lota watched them from her post by the flatbed. She was supposed to be keeping an eye on the western approach to the square, from the Birdman to the National Assembly steps, but when the dancing started up again, she kept getting pulled into the crowd—had to keep working her way back to the edge.

"Death to bad government!" Mad Max was shouting.

The crowd roared. Lota was swept sideways, like a leaf. It took her a while to regain her position, and when she did, she saw that Mad Max had disappeared, that Kurtz had risen in his place. She stood up there on the flatbed, lit up from behind by the high beams of a police van. Without speaking, without seeming to move or even breathe—watching everyone from above.

It wasn't until Bruno and Baby Jane jumped up behind her, partially blocking the light, that Mannie Groening laid down his trumpet and everyone stopped and looked up.

Kurtz's face was plunged almost completely into shadow so that only a few people, standing very near the truck, recognized her now. And when she did begin to speak, even with the help of the cordless microphone she carried, people didn't immediately seem to hear. They leaned in toward one another and asked, "Who is that?" or "What did she say?"

Even Lota, who was standing nearby, had to strain, at first. The microphone screeched. Then Bruno and Baby Jane stepped back; the light they'd blocked burst out in a brilliant flash.

"Cruelty and injustice," Kurtz said, her voice carrying now, the light framing her in a luminous glow. "Intolerance, oppression."

The murmur of the crowd grew to a rumble, then almost to a roar. "Sometimes," Kurtz said, "you have to take a leap of faith." The crowd exploded. Mannie Groening played a few licks on the trumpet. "The time for that leap is now," Kurtz said.

The music erupted; the dancing began. Instantly, Lota was swept into the crowd. She tried hard to push her way back to the edge. She pulled and shoved, tore blindly at people both in front and behind, but it was no use. The crowd had her firmly in its grip; it refused to release her.

She gave up. She *tried* to give up—to allow herself, like the moment itself, to simply exist, cut off from any seeming direction. She stretched out her hand and let it be clasped in passing. She felt the electric shock of contact. She stumbled, nearly fell, was lifted up.

The future is this, she thought. Is here. Is carrying me along . . .

Another hand reached out and she took it. But the pressure was different this time. Her whole body tensed; she tried and failed to retract her hand.

"Haroooooooooo!"

It was her brother Miles. His head swung dangerously in her direction and his eyes were lit up—nearly yellow, like a crow's. "Can you believe this?" he shouted.

Lota could smell his breath—it was strangely sweet. Again she attempted to release her hand.

"Can you fucking *believe this*?"

Lota yanked her hand hard and managed to free herself—but Miles caught her by the sleeve. She was no longer thinking about getting back to the edge and only wished, desperately, that she could lose herself again in the crowd. She didn't want to have to hold Miles's hand, to shake her head at him, to say, "No, I don't fucking believe it!"

A hard lump formed in her throat. She lurched forward—but Miles's grip was solid; he righted her.

"You okay?"

Lota doubled over again and heaved, but nothing came. Miles continued to hold on. He floated—a dark shadow above her. A dark shadow with yellow eyes. Yes, he and everyone else in the whole world, Lota thought, allowed themselves to float, to be simply pushed along, when she—alone—could not.

"You okay, little sister?" Miles asked.

In the eighth grade, Lota remembered, she had a teacher with hair nearly as red as her grandmother's had been and a thick mainland accent Lota had tried to imitate for a while. She hadn't even known she was doing it until her family said, "What's wrong with you?" Her mother had forced her mouth open to see if anything had got stuck down her throat.

The teacher—her name was Miss Everly—had told them a story about crabs in a bucket. If you put crabs in a bucket they will try to climb out, Miss Everly had said. But the crabs on the bottom will keep pulling the crabs at the top down into the bucket, so instead of a few, or all, of the crabs getting up to the top of the bucket, none of the crabs will get out.

At the end of the story, Miss Everly asked the class what they thought the story was about.

"*Crabs*," said Dex, in the row next to her. He emphasized the word in a way that made it sound dirty, and everybody laughed.

Miss Everly shrugged. "Yes and no," she told Dex.

It wasn't until years later, when she heard the story a second time and understood it right away, that she realized she hadn't understood it the first time.

But it wasn't the story (how she understood it then or later) that mattered to her in that moment—or the reason it floated back to her as she bent over double in the street. It was how Miss Everly had stood at the front of the class and looked at them with an expression that was, at the same time, both disappointed and bored. How—in the same accent that Lota had failed to imitate, which had sent her mother down her throat convinced that something was choking her—she'd said "Yes and no," and then, after a brief pause: "*You decide.*"

Of course Miles couldn't believe what was happening! When he'd told her about Kurtz and Black Zero three years ago, he'd acted like it was some sort of joke. And yet here they were. The future had arrived. They were free to move in any direction they chose; free to stumble, to trip over one another, to be pushed and pulled in any direction, without aim or desire.

Lota heaved again, and this time tasted bile. It'd been a damn lie, she thought. Miss Everly, the crabs, all of it. You couldn't just "decide"! It didn't work like that. She reached out to steady herself and grazed the shoulder of a passing stranger. You could only . . . blunder along. Be pushed forward and then backward, into whatever space opened before you; into whatever space, ahead of you, happened not to already be filled.

She heaved a third time, and a rush of sour-tasting liquid splashed onto the pavement and the toes of her boots. Everyone but Miles jumped back.

"Oh ho! You okay there, Sister?"

He stood there above her, swinging his head, his eyes glinting in the light. Then the darkness that ringed the square pressed in and her vision narrowed. Miles drifted farther and farther away. His eyes dimmed, his voice echoed strangely in the distance.

"Hey there, Sister! *Sis!*"

She saw a light, tapering at the bottom like the pattern of sweat she'd followed that morning, on Verbal's back.

Her head pounded. The light flashed brighter—then it, too, dimmed. If she could just keep it in sight, she thought—just keep following it this time . . .

She collapsed, her hands reaching toward the absent light. Miles caught her awkwardly before she hit the ground. He shook her, slapping at her cheeks. "Sister! *Sis!* Wake up, you hear me! You all right?"

Lota blinked. The world adjusted itself; the past receded. She opened her eyes and saw only her own knees, bent up nearly to her chin; saw Miles's thin arm, the lights from the police van, and a few shadowy forms hovering overhead. Everything, including the music, the heat, and the smell of her own vomit, felt too loud and close.

"Sis!"

Someone handed her a bottle of water. Miles tilted it to her lips and she drank. The water spilled out, splashing on her face and chest. It felt good. She drank some more. Then she got up unsteadily, spat. Her head was beating painfully, but she felt all right.

She turned back toward the flatbed. Mad Max seemed to be speaking, but she couldn't hear what he was saying over the music and the noise. She turned toward Miles, but he was looking at the flatbed—at the black flag Kurtz had hoisted there, with its central white circle—a zero, or an atoll. Something out of nothing, or was it the other way around? The end, or the beginning.

He seemed drawn to it, and in another moment he was gone—pulled into the crowd. Lota glimpsed his head bobbing along, not far off. It was a distance of little more than a pace or two, but she couldn't have reached him if she'd tried, and then she was no longer even entirely sure it was him she was looking at.

She let herself be thrust along—driven by the impulsive movements of the dancers. She watched the flag above the flatbed, concentrating on its white centre. She tried to move toward it, like Miles, but felt herself being pushed backward instead. She willed herself to focus, but everything felt blurred and out of joint. The horizon line seemed to tilt toward her, as though everything was bending back on itself. The future, she realized—and another sick wave passed over her—no longer stretched ahead of them. It pressed in. It surrounded them on every side.

The thought was interrupted by a powerful jolt from behind. A shout went up. Lota felt herself being grabbed and pulled; she stumbled, fell to one knee. For a panicked moment she thought she would go under.

Directly beneath her someone yelled, "*Help!*" Lota could hear the cry distinctly but she couldn't trace its source. It was as if the earth itself had cried out.

An alarm blared for half a minute or more, then cut out. Lota managed to right herself and realized, with horror, that her right knee had been pressed against a woman's back, pinning her to the ground. She leaned down and helped the woman up. Bewildered, and without acknowledging Lota, the woman shuffled away.

The flag hung listlessly in the distance. Lota could just make it out, lit up by the high beams of the police van.

"What the hell?" It was Miles again, swimming—unaccountably—back into view.

"A kid," someone said.

"Marty," someone else said, nearer. "Marty McDougall."

"Is he all right?" It was Miles. "Can you see anything?"

"God help us!"

"What's going on?"

The crowd contracted. Someone yelled, "Stay back!" Again Lota was pushed. Again she faltered, almost fell.

"Who the hell was driving?" Miles said.

"What happened?"

"A kid. Lily and Darrel's little boy."

"Hurt?"

"Dead, I think."

"Dead!"

A hush fell over the crowd. They could hear a woman begin to moan loudly. Lota looked around. Everyone who, a moment before, had been nearly stupid with joy was now equally dumb with confusion and fear. Someone had lost control of a car, she heard somebody say. Lily and Darrel's little boy had been hit badly. He was dead, someone said. No, he was alive, said someone else.

People who'd fallen got up slowly and dusted themselves off. Nobody knew what to do and so they just stood there, looking around, waiting for clues. Lota almost found herself wishing the crowd would press in on her again—sweep her and the moaning woman and the little boy away. She almost wished that without knowing where they were going, or why, they could be pulled and pushed together again, in all directions. Because, just as mere moments before, when Mannie Groening played the trumpet and everyone shivered and shook, moving their feet and shoulders and hips in time to the beat, there was nothing to do now but give in to what was happening—to watch and be carried by forces and events quite beyond their control.

But now this fact weighed heavily upon all of them.

A few people asked questions or cried a little, but mostly they stood in silence and watched as the kid got lifted into the car that had hit him. The car revved, a space was cleared for it. It drove away.

When it was gone, there was a moment of disturbed silence—then Mannie Groening raised his trumpet to his lips and played a few mournful notes. It was not at all clear to Lota as she watched and listened when these brief notes became a phrase, or the phrase a song. It was not clear at what point the other musicians lifted their instruments, or when—out of sheer relief—the first shout went up and the celebration resumed.

FOURTEEN

Rachel was sitting on the floor again, listening to music drift up from the street—to the odd, distant shout. There was no moon, and the brilliant glare of a single street lamp through her window made the night sky appear darker, even more absolute. She tried to raise herself high enough to glimpse the embassy yard, but even straining she was still too low to make out anything but the lamp and the empty sky.

She pushed against the desk and the drawer slid to its limit, then stuck. She tugged again, uselessly. The drawer didn't budge. If she could just manage to pull from a different angle. From above or below, rather than straight on . . .

Yes, that was it. Why hadn't she thought of it before? It *was* possible to unhook the drawer from the inside; she knew it for a fact. On her very first day in the office she'd slid it out completely in order to dump the debris (paper clips, pencil shavings, and, horribly, a few small, hardened crumbs of food) left behind by a former occupant. It had resisted at first, but after a few shakes, the drawer had shot out cleanly, as though there had never been a catch. What was difficult, she recalled, was getting the drawer back in again. She'd spent a good ten minutes attempting to line up the edges before it would slide smoothly back inside.

Rachel scooted as far as she could, until her back brushed the far wall. She shut her eyes and yanked down hard. Her wrists burned; the drawer wobbled.

She inched closer—keeping her arms extended this time so that the drawer didn't slide. She pressed her feet firmly against the back legs of the desk and gave the drawer another sharp downward tug. It sprang loose and fell with a clatter to the floor. Pens, paper clips, a flurry of envelopes, some sticky notes, and a few of her own business cards scattered.

Rachel picked up the drawer with her bound wrists and gave it a quick shake. A few more stray bits of paper fluttered, unhurriedly, to the ground. Her wrists throbbed painfully, but they didn't seem to bother her now. She held the drawer above her head like a trophy; felt happy, exhilarated—free.

Too quickly, the feeling faded. She lowered the drawer to her lap, flexed her wrists, and—without caring any longer who did or did not hear her—howled.

So the drawer was no longer attached to the desk, but her hands were still attached to the drawer; her pants were still wet; she was thirsty, hungry, and trapped on a remote island without any sign of help.

She'd begun to sweat and now, for the first time, she realized that the air conditioning had been turned off. So that was why the building felt so quiet and strange. She'd never been in the building without the air conditioning on and so had never realized how loud it was—or that it was possible to miss something you'd never even heard.

The silence began to bother her. Why, she wondered, had no one answered her shout?

Without actually deciding to do so, Rachel began moving toward the door. She progressed slowly at first, painfully, but even so, once she was on her way, the idea did not seem such a bad one. Didn't she owe it to herself at least to try?

Try *what*? Her mind raced. Surely, she thought, there was something to be done if she could only just think of it. If she could talk to the ambassador; find out what he knew and what he didn't . . .

Rachel felt a flutter of panic in her chest. She hadn't quite worked out what she'd tell the ambassador about her own encounters with the insurgents.

Well, she'd simply have to tell him the truth, wouldn't she? As shameful as it was. This thing was bigger than her. How she came off looking was not really the point.

She shifted the drawer slightly to her left and lunged forward on all fours. *Good*. She was almost to the door.

It had been a long time since she'd pictured recounting anything of what was happening to her—a long time since she'd done anything, or had a single thought, that was worthy of report—but she pictured it now. "Of course I was scared," she imagined telling Ray. "I was nearly out of my mind. But there comes a point when fear turns into something else, when it doesn't matter anymore."

With a little manoeuvring, Rachel managed to wedge a foot between the door and the wall, opening it wide enough to pass.

She pictured Ray, leaning in, his look saying both "You surprise me!" and "I should have guessed." "There's a certain autonomy," she'd inform him, "an innate sort of optimism, in losing all hope."

Outside, the only light came from a window on the third-floor landing and the Exit signs that glowed at each end of the hall. Rachel looked left first, past the storage and copy rooms, then right, toward Fred Bradley's office, and the ambassador's.

Yes, the ambassador, Rachel thought, as she headed down the hall. He'd know what to do. Or at least he'd know what needed to be secured—and how to secure it. He'd know how to locate and erase certain files. If things started to look really bad (the thought flashed before Rachel suddenly—nearly dazzled her) they could simply burn the building down.

But that was getting a bit drastic, wasn't it? Rachel gritted her teeth and shoved herself another few feet down the hall. In any case, she couldn't simply sit around any longer and wait—especially when she was no longer sure what exactly she was waiting for.

She could still hear the shouts, the music, drifting up from the street—the distant sounds of a victory being celebrated that could not (despite all evidence) actually have been won.

And yet, what else could she assume at this point?

She passed Bradley's door—shut tight. Rachel hesitated in front of it, nearly tapped it with her foot. But something stopped her. It would be better, she considered, to go straight to the ambassador. Besides, there was something that had always disturbed her a little about Bradley. There was something a bit . . . too calm about him, as if he'd already anticipated everything. Even before you could finish a sentence, he'd be murmuring, "Right, right," like he knew exactly what you were going to say. It was on account of trying too hard to please, of course—but, still, it came out wrong. Dismissive and condescending.

She continued down the hall with the drawer in front of her now, like a sort of crutch. She made even more noise this way and once or twice she stopped to listen, her ears pricked for any sound coming from either inside or outside of the building that indicated she'd been heard.

Nothing. Nothing from Bradley's office or from the ambassador's—and nothing from outside except for the same drifting strains of music and voices.

Finally, Rachel reached the ambassador's door. She hesitated—suddenly unsure. Then, the drawer dragging painfully, she lifted her wrists and knocked twice.

No answer. What did she expect? Rachel turned the knob and pushed—harder than she needed to. The door swung open and she tumbled into the ambassador's office, the drawer slamming hard against the tile.

The ambassador was seated on the floor in the corner of the room, his wrists cuffed to the leg of his desk. He looked clouded and unkempt—like one of the old men stationed at nearly all hours outside of Josie's canteen—and didn't seem to immediately recognize Rachel.

"Hello, Kinsley," Rachel said, righting herself as best she could.

"Darling?"

"Yes!"

"Darling. What the hell?" The ambassador's teeth chattered.

"Listen, Kinsley," Rachel said. "I need to tell you . . ."

The ambassador stared at her, his teeth still chattering.

"They *know.*"

The ambassador continued to stare.

Rachel forced herself to continue. "They know," she said, and took a deep breath. "About the maps, and everything. Where to find them. And . . . and about the station, too. They mentioned something about it. Something about . . . extraordinary renditions."

The ambassador blinked.

"It might be all nonsense, of course, but I wanted to make sure, and I thought that maybe . . ." Again she felt uncertain—ridiculous, even. She realized that, if the ambassador wasn't going to supply her with any more information—regarding what exactly the insurgents were looking for and where they were going to find it—she herself had nothing to propose. "That maybe . . . it would be wise—"

"I know one of them, you know," the ambassador interrupted. Despite how earnestly she'd hoped that the ambassador would speak, the interruption startled Rachel. Even more surprising was that, despite his unkempt appearance and chattering teeth, the ambassador's voice was his own. Loud, competent, nonchalant—a slight trace of a country accent he'd worked hard to either cultivate or erase. "Yes, hard to believe," the ambassador continued, "but she's one of our own. From Intelligence. I worked with her years ago. She was just starting out." He sniffed, wiped at his nose with his shirt. "She was talented," he said. "Very, very bright. Worked her way right up the ranks—too quickly, probably. Took on a few too many tough jobs and started to crack. I heard later she'd been demoted—but she knew too much by then to be entirely let go. They took her out of the system, made her invisible. *My* guess," the ambassador said with a short laugh, "is she's started to resent that."

He closed his eyes tight, his big pale cheeks pressed up to his bushy eyebrows, which he more regularly combed, his jaw clenched so his teeth couldn't chatter. When he opened his eyes again he looked inhumanly tired. "You know," he said slowly—accentuating the barely detectable drawl—"Bradley's dead."

"What?" Rachel lurched forward. A large bead of perspiration dripped conspicuously from her forehead onto the floor. "*What?*" she said again, though she'd heard the ambassador perfectly well.

The shots; yes. She'd heard them—felt them, even. Had *known* they were close, she couldn't help *that*. And yet, she still had somehow never imagined! Had only supposed . . .

Supposed what? That the gun had been directed at no one? That there'd been—and *would* be—no consequences?

"*What?*" Rachel said a third time.

The ambassador shrugged. His expression suggested unconcern, even indifference, but when he opened his mouth his teeth were still chattering. "They told me it was an accident. That he pulled a gun."

"*Bradley?*"

"I know." A high-pitched squeak. The ambassador attempted to cover his mouth with his wrists. "It's difficult to picture."

Rachel stared at him. Had the man actually *giggled*? Also: why in the hell had Bradley been carrying a gun?

"We need to destroy the documents," Rachel said, uncertainly.

"What documents?" The ambassador's face had gone blank again. He sniffed loudly.

"The . . . the maps!" Rachel exploded. "And anything that suggests . . . in terms of intelligence, anything at all . . . *extraordinary* . . ."

The ambassador once more wiped at his nose with his sleeve. He was not looking at Rachel; his expression remained neutral, impassive.

"They *know,*" Rachel repeated, a little desperately now. "They told me . . . They said that Phil, you know, had mentioned a connection . . ."

"Darling," the ambassador said, shaking his head. "Please. Try to relax."

"It's just . . ." Rachel felt offended, then confused. "It could all look very bad, sir. I mean, no doubt, from the outside . . ."

"Relax, Darling. The last thing we need is to lose our heads," the ambassador drawled. "Listen to me. None of this matters. No one will find anything. None of this even exists."

"But—" Rachel felt like she was going to burst into tears and had to swallow hard to keep her voice from breaking. "They said they'd been talking to Phil," she said. "I know they could have made it all up, but either way, sir . . ."

"*Darling!*"

Rachel sat up straight—blinked twice at the ambassador. Little droplets of sweat streamed down her face.

"I told you. Relax. Whatever they *know*—or think they know—it doesn't matter. This isn't Empire soil, is it? You have to remember that. Whatever happens here, we're not responsible. I promise you. The maps are another dead end. They can't possibly do anything with them without Ø, and Ø can't do a thing without us. It all leads nowhere, you see? To nothing. We've simply got to wait."

"Yes. Yes, I understand," Rachel said, even though she didn't understand. "But in the meantime . . ."

"There is no meantime, Darling."

Rachel looked wildly around the room, as if hoping to seek another opinion somewhere. She coughed. Attempted to clear her throat. "You said . . . you said he pulled a gun."

"What?"

"Bradley," Rachel almost shouted. "You said he pulled a gun."

The ambassador shrugged. "That's what I was told."

Rachel leaned forward. "Do you think," she said—lowering her voice—"do you think he killed someone?"

Again the ambassador shrugged, slouching against the leg of his desk. Rachel's heart beat audibly. She took a few deep breaths. Then the ambassador wondered aloud what time it was in the capital and Rachel's thoughts drifted painfully toward Zoe and Ray. She tried to picture them—going about their ordinary day, both of them still oblivious, perhaps.

"Nearly noon, I'd say," the ambassador suggested.

She pictured Ray grabbing an umbrella on his way out the door for a meeting, or lunch with a friend. Zoe struggling with the zipper on her coat, balling up her paper lunch sack, or standing in line for the swings.

With a twinge of guilt, Rachel recalled that the ambassador was a recent divorcee. His wife had left him a year ago—gone back to the capital. They had no children. What, she wondered, was the ambassador thinking about now? What, she wondered —beginning to panic a little at the thought—was there to sustain anyone, at any time, if not Zoe? Ray?

Again, she saw Ray. Making his way down the short path from the office to the street; unlocking his vehicle; straightening his jacket at the neck and the shoulders before ducking inside. She felt deeply sorry for anyone who, in that moment, could not likewise picture the slant of his forehead or the tendons in his neck as he glanced quickly behind him; his long fingers on the wheel.

The ambassador's head lolled. Rachel stole a peek at his crotch; it looked dry. How was that even possible?

She should leave, of course; Rachel knew that. Make her way back to her own office—and fast. There was nothing to be done here, that was obvious. She'd been a fool to think, even for a moment, she should try.

"It all leads nowhere," the ambassador had said.

And here was Rachel, putting them both at needless risk. For god's sake, Bradley was already dead!

She should leave; should make her way back as quickly as she could, slide the desk drawer back into place as though it had never been removed . . . And yet, for some reason, she lingered. She'd never been particularly fond of the ambassador—had found him irritatingly self-important, affected, aloof. And yet, perhaps precisely for this reason, his presence was at least a small comfort to her now. She admired the way he could still be neutral, offhand—even while his teeth chattered. He'd come up at the tail end of an era where a slap on the back and a stiff drink solved just about anything—and it showed. By the time Rachel and Ray had come along everything was different. They'd learned to be more cautious, more sober. Rachel stuck her foot in her mouth more; Ray—for fear of it—said nothing at all.

Not long ago, Ray had recounted to Rachel a conversation he'd had with a retired counsellor. "It's the women," the counsellor had told him. "Forgive my saying so, but they seem to muck up absolutely everything." He'd waved a long arm and sloshed his drink in his glass. "I know it's not exactly PC to say so, is it? But truly. We used to—you know—be able to get right *down* to it, you know, and now you literally can't say a thing without *someone* objecting."

It seemed that Ray expected Rachel to be outraged at this—personally incensed.

"You sound surprised," she'd said. "You sound like you didn't realize this is what all the old men are thinking. At least he deemed you worthy to be spoken to. *I* try to talk to one of those guys and their eyes glaze over."

Ray stared at her blankly.

"You never noticed that?" Rachel asked. "Whenever we're out together somewhere, you know they only speak to you."

Ray looked confused. No, he said, he could honestly say he hadn't noticed. But now that she mentioned it, he said, maybe she was right. It was true that, whereas he was always hyper-visible in diplomatic gatherings, standing out awkwardly like a sore thumb, Rachel tended to fade a little, to *blend in*.

"I'm sorry," Ray said, but he didn't look sorry. He looked embarrassed—annoyed, even.

Rachel shrugged. She refused to let it bother her. "Don't worry," she said. "Those guys are going to all die out sooner or later. It's a natural process." She winked at Ray. "You may have even heard of it? It's called *evolution*."

And now here, perhaps, Rachel thought glumly, was the last of them. The ambassador's head had dropped to his chest, revealing a patch of thinning hair on top and the beginnings of a double chin. In point of fact, Rachel and the ambassador were separated by little more than a decade and a half—and yet, in generational terms, they were worlds apart. At best, Rachel could only imitate what for the ambassador seemed to come so naturally: the cool, unshakable disposition, the innate distrust of anything, or anyone, he didn't already know.

Maybe this was really it, Rachel thought—the end. In another few moments, right here in this room, the ambassador was going to be wiped off the face of the earth and with him the very last of a generation.

What had she said to Ray again? *Evolution*. The natural progression of things. There wasn't anything that either one of them could do about it now. She might as well follow the ambassador's example: *relax*. There was, after all, something seriously compelling about the way the ambassador had managed to remain confidently oblivious even while being scared almost out of his wits. About the way his fear had remained simple and discrete, at the root of it only the most basic of questions: was he or was he not going to die? The question had throbbed through the room like a foot tapping, had finally lulled him to sleep.

Rachel could feel her own eyelids begin to droop. Remarkably, the possibility of sleep presented itself to her. It extended itself—a simple offering. But just as she was about to reach out and take it, she heard the sharp sound of boots ringing on the stairs below, and she was wide awake again. She looked across at the ambassador, who didn't stir—felt a cold panic spread like pins and needles through her limbs.

She'd left it too late; there was no time now. No time to return, no time to slide the drawer back in place—to pretend that she'd never left. Rachel cursed herself fiercely.

What had she been thinking? Putting not only her own life in danger but the life of the ambassador, and the others as well?

The footsteps were almost at the landing now. A loud shout, then a laugh, echoed in the stairwell.

It was, after all, Rachel thought sadly, quite impossible to take only your own life in hand.

More footsteps. The squeak of boots on the stair.

Still the ambassador hadn't stirred. Rachel listened again and attempted to gauge what direction the footsteps were moving in and how much time she still had before they reached the ambassador's door.

FIFTEEN

Lota sat next to Norma in the basement conference centre at the Bella Vista Hotel. Her headache had returned; the laptop screen in front of her glared. She stared around at the others. At Mad Max hugging his rifle, at Bruno staring blearily at the ceiling, at Baby Jane tugging at a strand of blond hair. Of all of them, Kurtz was the only one who seemed not to notice they'd been up since dawn without a proper meal or a moment's rest. She paced the room feverishly. Her skin shone, her eyes glowed; she seemed physically taller, as if she actually took up more space. But then, at the same time, her edges had softened—begun to blur. It was as if, Lota thought, she'd become an element among them rather than a human being—had begun to slowly diffuse into the atmosphere.

Lota turned back to the screen, but she couldn't focus on it properly. The letters appeared indistinct and strangely elongated. They didn't seem to be arranged in any immediately recognizable order.

She looked up again and was surprised to see Verbal. He stood toward the front of the room; Kurtz almost grazed his shoulder as she passed.

Lota's heart gave a sick, sideways leap. So it had all, she thought, been a dream. So there was still time to go back, do it over again. She felt relieved, but also exhausted by the thought. She shook her head. Surely her eyes were playing tricks on her . . .

But even after blinking three times hard, and rubbing her eyes, Verbal remained—hovering in the space between the cheap maplewood lectern and the wall. He faced her without exactly looking at her, his eyes with that weird expression in them, as though he was searching for something beyond her that she could neither see nor understand.

Then his eyes seemed to brighten—to sharpen at the edges. Slowly, they began to drift toward hers.

A hard lump formed in Lota's throat. She stared, transfixed, as Verbal's eyes continued to drift. Yes, it was inevitable, now, that their eyes would meet. Lota could not turn her head. A wave—first of horror and then of intense desire—passed over her. And then (because she was suddenly unsure which feeling was which, or if the two feelings were actually one) she was hit by a still more powerful wave of confusion. It was possible, Lota thought regretfully, that she didn't want any second chances—didn't want to go back.

By the time Verbal's gaze reached hers, he was gone.

"Hey, snap out of it." It was Norma, beside her.

Lota winced. She glanced back at the screen, but the words of the document still appeared smudged and blurred.

It should have been simple, of course: after all, the story had already been written. Lota's job was simply to copy and paste it into separate email files.

"You all right?"

Lota bit her lip. Her vision sharpened slightly. She squinted, straining to make out the words on the screen.

A BRIGHT NEW DAWN FOR ISLAND NATION.

"I'm all right," she said.

Kurtz was still pacing. Lota scanned the document. This time, for the most part, the letters stayed in place on the page. She managed to get nearly halfway through before her eyes snagged.

"Look," Lota said in a low voice to Norma, "it says here . . ." But then she faltered. She didn't know if what she wanted to ask was a question, exactly.

Norma was hunched over her own screen. She was compiling a list of email addresses and didn't look up.

"It says here," Lota began again, "at the beginning of the third paragraph: 'Not a single shot was fired.'"

Norma continued to tap at the keyboard, her eyes—obscured by the slant of her cap—fixed straight ahead on the screen.

"I was wondering . . ." Again, Lota paused.

What exactly *was* she wondering? What revision *now*, after the fact, would possibly suffice? The thing was done. The story had already been written.

"This is an official statement," Norma said, still without looking up. "It's not intended to give a complete report." She leaned back a little in her foldout chair so that its two front legs were raised slightly off the floor. Then she rocked forward with a sudden jolt. "You ready?"

She'd turned toward Lota and smiled. For once the smile did not seem ironic, but friendly—almost kind. Mostly out of gratitude, Lota found herself nodding. The words, and her response to them, seemed now, in any case, to have little meaning.

Norma hit Send. Lota clicked to her inbox and waited for the message to appear. When it did, she copy-and-pasted the addresses Norma had sent her into the BCC box of a new message. Then she copy-and-pasted the press release and turned to stare blankly at Norma. But Norma wasn't looking at her. She'd already waved to Kurtz—was watching as Kurtz moved toward them quickly, surrounded by a hazy glow.

It was her auntie G who'd taught Lota to read. Even before she'd even started school, Auntie G had helped her trace the letters of the alphabet on transparent paper. Lota could still recall the pressure of her auntie's fingers on her own, the smell of the freshly sharpened pencil, the barely detectable sound of the letter taking shape on the page. "She's too young," her mother had said, "you're wasting your time." But Auntie G had just shrugged. Later, she'd said to Lota, "You're never too young to learn to pay attention. See, once you know the letters, it's just a matter of looking for connections—for certain patterns, for the way the patterns tend to repeat."

Kurtz was behind her now, peering over Lota's shoulder at the screen. Lota could feel the pressure, the heat from her body. She looked up. Kurtz nodded. Lota pressed Send.

There was a small whoosh and the browser automatically closed. Incredulously, Lota stared at the blank screen. She tried to imagine the words she'd copied disassembling—invisibly—being conducted underwater on their way to the capital and at least twenty-seven other destinations all over the world.

It was—what? She looked at the time at the top of the screen. 4:44 A.M. on a day that, in the capital, had not even dawned.

The air conditioner hummed noisily. Lota closed her eyes and little bright lights danced on the insides of her eyelids. When she opened them she saw that Kurtz had returned to the front of the room. She was standing between the lectern and the wall, in exactly the same place where, a half-hour before, Lota had seen Verbal.

"Are you ready?" Kurtz panned the room with her gaze. "In under a minute," she said, "I'm going to have the phones ringing off the hook." She flipped her own phone open and raised a finger in the air as if testing the direction of the wind.

Nobody said anything. A few silently nodded.

Then Mad Max pushed through the door carrying three plastic water pitchers. He set the pitchers down in the middle of the room on a table that—for some unknown and now quite unimaginable reason—had been draped in a shiny mauve tablecloth. A line formed in front of the pitchers, which Lota joined.

She stood with the others as they took turns pouring and then repouring water into little plastic cups.

Bruno's phone rang. He stepped away from the table. "Yes, hello?"

Then it was Hannibal's turn; then Killmonger's; then Baby Jane's. "Hello? Yes—that's correct. The island is now under local authority and control."

"Hello?" It was Lota's turn now.

"After over three hundred years of systemic oppression . . ."

"We have risen to our feet . . ."

"The island is now . . ."

"Yes, hello?"

"Hello—"

"Because it is better to sacrifice everything . . ."

Lota tried to keep her eyes on her script. To read the whole thing through without stumbling or making a single mistake. The telephones buzzed and rang. Kurtz paced the room, sipping water from plastic cups, then destroying them. Their voices rose and fell, interrupting each other, repeating themselves at staggered intervals:

"We consent to everything for it . . ."

"We have risen to our feet . . ."

"After over three hundred years of systemic oppression . . ."

"We aspire to live and die as equals . . ."

"Because it is better to sacrifice everything . . ."

"We consent . . ."

The phones had stopped ringing. The breaking-news reports had entered circulation: the story had been written. It was out of their hands.

Kurtz and Mad Max left the room and there was a strange silence as the rest of them—awaiting orders and drugged with fatigue—sat slouched over the mauve tablecloth.

A minute or two ticked by like that. Then, with a swift, angry motion, Norma scraped her chair back from the table. She crossed the room in a few quick steps and left through the open door. Mr. Joshua followed. Lota looked up briefly as they departed, then back to the table. She was drifting. Possibly she was already asleep.

But then there was Baby Jane beside her. She'd pulled up a chair and sat down in it heavily, her arms folded. For a minute she just sat there like that looking at Lota, sucking at both cheeks.

Finally: "It will kill Melea," she said. Her voice was tense, but it didn't waver. "You," she said. "You'll be all right—you're young. But it will kill Melea."

Lota shook her head. "It was a mistake," she said, her voice rising. "An accident."

"I'm not asking you to explain."

"One of them. He had a gun!"

Baby Jane rolled her neck to one side slowly, watching Lota carefully the whole time, as though trying to figure her out—or make up her mind.

Then she dropped her arms from her chest. "He was *everything* to Melea," she said. Her voice was a whisper, barely audible above the hum of the air conditioning and the overhead fan. "But he wasn't her son—he was *hers*." She nodded toward the door.

Lota followed her gaze. She blinked. Her head felt funny.

"Yes, that's right," Baby Jane hissed. She leaned closer. "Verbal was *hers*, was *Kurtz's* boy. He never knew it, of course. She and Melea both—they wanted it that way. He was just a baby when she left. It was only natural that Melea would raise him."

Baby Jane took a deep breath, as if she'd been underwater. She rocked back and looked at Lota, her eyes squinting slightly. Nearly ten seconds ticked by.

Lota betrayed nothing. She sat still as a statue. She didn't even blink.

Baby Jane watched her carefully all that time. Then, as if she'd detected something in Lota that Lota herself couldn't guess at, she nodded approvingly. "You see, Melea," Baby Jane whispered, shaking her head, "she never had any children of her own. She was always worried because of it—worried that Kurtz would come back. Take her baby away."

Lota pressed her mouth into a tight line and looked back at Baby Jane without really seeing her. For the first time, she noticed the absolute and wholly impenetrable reality of the objects that surrounded her. For example, the singular existence of the chair beneath her. Of the table. The wrinkled curtains. The emptied water pitchers, the clock on the wall. She felt a dull sort of panic and glanced around quickly, as though for a way out. But there was no way out. There was only, as far as she could see, one object upon another—all the way down. The windows. The fluorescent light bulbs. The scrub grass outside.

A shadow appeared in the door. Lota looked up. It was Kurtz. She stood with her hands on her hips, her feet planted firmly a good two feet apart, her chin jutted, her eyes like two stones.

Lota looked at her. As if for the first time, she looked at her. Like she was an emptied water pitcher, or a chair, or a clock on the wall.

"Mercer broke," Kurtz said. "We've got the code."

SIXTEEN

The voices were almost upon them before the ambassador woke. He started, his eyes flew open. He stared directly past Rachel, in the direction of the door—his face utterly blank. Rachel had inched her way back, had pressed herself as near as she was able against the adjacent wall, but the office was not large, and when the door burst open and a man and a woman walked in, she was sitting almost directly beneath them.

"Hello, hello!" the man said. He was evidently drunk and held onto the edge of the door as he entered the room. The woman pushed past him. She was about a head shorter than the man and thin as a rail, but she looked tougher somehow. She wore a checkered newsboy cap pulled down low over her eyes and two long braids down the middle of her back.

"Hold on!" the woman said. The man had looked right past Rachel, toward the ambassador, but the woman had immediately caught sight of her—was crouched beside her now, peering at her from under the brim of her hat. "What's this now?" the woman said in a loud voice. "Am I seeing double?"

The man was holding on to the doorknob with one hand and adjusting the bandana he wore on his head, Rambo-style, with the other. He still hadn't seen Rachel—even though if he'd taken another step he would have stepped on her.

"Oh ho! What's this?" he said when he finally did see her. He leaned over the crouching woman, reeking of alcohol and sour sweat. Only the desk drawer was between Rachel and him. "You looking to ek-scape?"

Rachel had intended to shake her head, but for some reason all she could manage was a single turn—a reflexive motion as if she'd been slapped.

"Look at me," the man said.

Rachel turned her head painfully.

The man began to laugh loudly. Then, stumbling a little, he moved to the door, shut it, and reclined against the glass.

Rachel glanced at the ambassador, who was still staring around, not really *at* anything—a look on his face like whatever was happening he already knew about, had already foreseen.

Yes, he was indeed a rare old breed, Rachel thought. But now, instead of being comforted, she began to feel frightened by the ambassador's extreme reserve, his blank, omniscient stare. She wished, again—desperately—that she'd never left her own office. She didn't want to die with the ambassador looking on like that. Like he already knew everything that was about to happen; like he had nothing personally at stake.

For the first time in her life, Rachel prayed. Briefly, violently, without any real hope, or forethought, or even words.

The woman got up slowly, still staring at Rachel. She dragged over a chair and sat down in it carefully, crossing one thin leg over the other and adjusting her hat so that, though Rachel could still feel the woman's eyes on her, she could no longer see them. "I think these two have some explaining to do," she said.

Her companion nodded. "You're going to have to answer for yourselves sooner or later," he said. Then he kicked at the drawer a little, wrenching Rachel's wrists badly.

"You know, don't you," the ambassador said in a flat voice—very empty and calm—"this is all very silly."

His eyes, when Rachel looked at them, were nearly opaque.

"Whatever you're after," the ambassador continued coolly, "you simply won't succeed in finding it. You *can't*."

Far from soothing her, the ambassador's words sounded hollow to Rachel—dangerously false.

"According to our country's chief security officer . . ." the ambassador continued.

Rachel's stomach twisted.

". . . in five years—maybe even less—the entire world . . ."

The man had begun pacing the corner of the room, but now he lurched violently toward the ambassador. "What do you want with us, anyway?" He practically shouted the question, but the ambassador didn't even flinch. "What do you want with us?" the man repeated. He was looking in the woman's direction now, as though seeking approval or support. "What *is* this place to you?" he said, turning back to the ambassador. "A place to bury your secrets? To hide?"

His gaze drifted back to the woman.

"And we're supposed to do what?" he shouted—more at her now than anyone else. "Just wait? Until you blow it up again?"

"If there was any debt," the ambassador said calmly, although it didn't seem as though the man was talking to him anymore, "it's been more than repaid."

The man started. He gave his head a quick, violent shake. The woman—without shifting her position—released a short laugh.

The laugh seemed to trigger something in the man because, all at once, he lunged. He pressed his hands against the wall, his face hovering just inches above the ambassador's own. "We know what you do here," he said, and reached into the deep inside pocket of the zippered jacket he wore.

Involuntarily, Rachel reeled back, hitting her head against the wall. But it was only a small metal flask that the man had retrieved. He opened it and raised it suggestively. "What do you say?" he asked the room, generally. "Take the edge off?"

The ambassador must have nodded because the man began to pour the liquid out slowly; the ambassador opened his mouth like a bird.

"Twenty-seven foreign prisoners," the woman said in her surprisingly deep, clear voice. "Kept without documentation, or ever being charged with a crime. There's evidence, you know. Of torture. Of deprivation. Of every imaginable abuse and indiscretion."

"You won't succeed." The ambassador's eyes were glassy, his chin glistened.

The man screwed the lid on the flask and slammed his fist against the ambassador's desk. A stapler bounced and the pens and pencils in their holders rattled.

"You think this is about freedom, am I right?" the ambassador said. "About history, perhaps. Or religion? Well, it's not. I can tell you that right now. And you'll discover it yourself, too. Sooner or later."

"Goddamnyou!" The man pitched forward and grabbed the ambassador by the throat.

"Your leader, for example. If you think she's a *revolutionary* . . ." The ambassador choked a little, snorted through his nose. "Well. You'll find the truth out soon enough. She's a regular crook, you know. She's a spy."

"Goddamnyou!" The man closed his hands more firmly around the ambassador's throat, but the ambassador showed no sign of either distress or alarm.

He continued, gasping a little now: "She was one of ours once, you know . . ." Perhaps unconsciously, the man released some of the pressure from the ambassador's throat. "Oh, you didn't know that?" The ambassador coughed dryly. "She betrayed us. But that was a long time ago now. She will, almost certainly—"

But then the air cracked. It was less a sound than a physical blow. The woman, still reclined slightly in the office chair, had pulled her gun out and fired. A few full seconds ticked by before Rachel was able to confirm that no one had been hit. The bullet had entered the wall, just above the ambassador's head. The man looked—incredulously—at the hole in the wall, then at the ambassador, and then at the woman. He took a confused step toward her and held out his hand. But the woman had already fired again. With her companion out of the way, she aimed low. The bullet entered the ambassador's stomach, just below the chest. The force propelled the ambassador's body forward, but his eyes, uncannily, remained trained ahead—though he still did not appear to actually see anything.

Rachel yelled out, but no one paid her any attention now. The man had spun back, stumbling against a chair—then he righted himself. All three of them watched as blood unfurled itself in a brilliant red band.

There was a strange sound. A low hum that at first Rachel thought was coming from the ambassador—a sort of death rattle. But then the sound grew louder and she realized that it wasn't coming from inside the room at all. She risked a glance at the woman and then the man. They stood frozen, eyes tipped toward the ceiling—listening to, but not yet recognizing the sound.

Then—at once—they knew. Rachel watched as the woman's, expression changed slowly, betraying—What? Confusion, certainly. Anger. Fear. And . . . something else. A sort of (or was this only a projection?) instinctive, physical relief.

The sound grew louder. The woman got up slowly. She bent over the ambassador's body toward the window ledge and looked out. She craned her thin neck one way and then the other. Then she pushed herself abruptly from the ledge. Leaning toward the man, she said something Rachel could not make out.

The two of them hurried from the room. They swung the door behind them as they went, though not hard enough for it to actually close. Rachel could hear their muffled voices, the way their shoes squeaked against the tile floor.

She turned toward the ambassador expectantly. As if she believed he might look up suddenly, and—his eyes staring off at some fixed point in the middle distance—explain to her what was happening in that cool, calm voice that suggested he knew, ahead of time, the way things would go.

But the ambassador didn't look up. The sound outside continued to grow louder—had become, by now, a dull roar—but the ambassador didn't appear to be hearing it.

Rachel wanted to shout. She wanted to leap at him, give his shoulders a shake. Wake up! she wanted to yell. Wake up! You were right all along! We're *saved*! It was not just one or two planes she heard out there now; an entire air force seemed to be descending.

There might, she considered, as the noise roared closer, still even be time. She could stop up the ambassador's wound, maybe open an airway . . .

But she felt frozen—her back still pressed firmly against the wall. And then it was too late. She heard steps returning, echoing up the stairwell and along the hall. Her heart, already pounding, began to beat so fiercely that she felt certain it would burst. She pulled her knees up to her chest to contain it and felt something—a hard object in her pocket, digging sharply into her skin. Only then did she recall the necklace she'd picked up earlier that day: the snake curled into the shape of a hydrogen atom, seeming to eat its own tail. How stupid she'd been, she thought, as the footsteps drew nearer, how naive. To have thought that, from all this, something could be taken away.

The woman banged into the office again—alone this time. The cap she wore was pulled down low, but Rachel could just make out the strange pale glow of her eyes. She stared into that glow and was surprised to feel a little like how the ambassador had looked: oddly indifferent, aloof.

Because, it didn't matter! No, Rachel thought, none of it mattered anymore . . . Help *had* arrived. Just as the ambassador —and Rachel herself, deep down—had always known it would.

Only why, oh why, she couldn't help thinking, had it taken so long? Bradley was dead. So, no doubt, was the ambassador. And who knew what had happened to Phil, to everyone else . . .

But the thought dissipated quickly, was drowned out by the single-minded roar of the approaching aircraft—by their undeniable proximity and intent.

There must, after all, have been *some reason*. It would all—yes, and very soon now—be explained.

Yes, very soon, thought Rachel, as the woman, shrugging off Rachel's gaze, moved to the middle of the room, she herself would be on board one of those planes. Very soon now she'd be touching down in the capital. Very soon . . .

Tears of relief welled in Rachel's eyes. All of this, plus everything else she'd worried about over the past six months, and even longer than that, would be dissolved instantly—as Ray's arms wrapped around her shoulders, as she folded Zoe into her own.

The woman's eyes snapped up. She took a few quick steps toward the window and, leaning again across the ambassador, craned her neck to look up at the sky. The planes, Rachel thought, must be just overhead. She practically shook with joy —and yet, as she looked at the younger woman, whose face was hidden from her again now, she felt . . . sorry. Yes. That was it. She'd tell Ray as soon as she saw him. She felt goddamned sorry for all of it! Sorry for them all!

The woman spun round, her eyes under the brim of her cap flicking toward Rachel like the tongue of a snake. The two women stared at each other. The planes roared overhead.

Then the younger woman shot forward and, instinctively, Rachel reeled back. But she was too late and, anyway, there was nowhere to go. The younger woman had whipped her around in a stranglehold.

"Don't move, fool."

Rachel yelped from pain and surprise. But then she felt something cold and hard against her throat and froze.

Oh God, she thought, and inhaled sharply. *If this is the end . . .*

But it couldn't be. It couldn't. It was too cruel—too impossibly cruel. There was a tight feeling in Rachel's chest. She attempted to breathe without moving any of the muscles in her neck. The tight feeling spread slowly. It became a hard knot in her throat—a physical pressure against the sharp blade.

She could smell the other woman, could feel the sweat from her shirt, feel it begin to dampen her own.

"Please," Rachel said. "*Please—*"

The woman tightened her hold. "Quiet, fool."

Yes, Rachel thought. *Fool.* She'd been a fool. A fool to have doubted. A fool to have believed.

She could hear the other woman's heart beating—couldn't help it. The woman's chest was pressed up flat against Rachel's ear and it was beating like a jackhammer. Rachel listened. So she, too, Rachel thought, is afraid. She, too, is thinking how small she is in all of this and wondering what will come next. The thought should have comforted her, but it didn't.

Then the noise from the planes began to slowly fade. *Of course,* Rachel thought. They must be headed toward the landing site on the other end of the island.

The knot in her throat was nearly choking her now, but she didn't dare swallow. She felt the woman's grip tighten; felt the blade begin to tremble in her grasp. She felt her heart pounding, but then became momentarily confused because she didn't know for certain any longer if it was her own.

The woman's grip tightened still further; the blade wobbled; the planes in the distance droned their descent.

SEVENTEEN

At first the sound was indistinguishable from the hum of voices and the low drone of the AC. Lota sensed it before she could hear it. But then the noise sharpened slightly. Bruno lifted his head like a dog.

Then Mad Max heard it; then Hal; then Baby Jane. Their voices began to drop off. Lota's skin pricked. She felt empty inside—hollowed out, like a shell.

Finally, Kurtz. She stopped pacing and her eyes brightened. She turned toward the wall at the front of the room with its narrow strip of windows, though nothing much was visible out there. Only the dull grey sidewalk could be seen, with its little tufts of couch grass that continued to grow stubbornly through the cracks in the concrete.

Even so, Lota, along with all the rest of Kurtz's soldiers, followed her gaze. One by one they turned their heads. Lota, Hannibal, Alien, Killmonger, and Alex DeLarge. Then Hans, Mystique, Pinky, Khan. They peered together through the frosted glass as though there was actually something to see out there.

Then they turned back toward Kurtz, their eyes wide—expectant—waiting for some explanation, some command.

But Kurtz only continued to stare past them toward the strip of windows and the wall. She stretched her arms out toward the sidewalk, the couch grass, the dull orange glow that had just begun to lick at the edges of the cracked stone. Her eyes blazed. For a moment, she seemed to *burn*. Then she let her arms fall and turned abruptly toward the exit. She crossed the room without once looking back.

The soldiers stared after her, wondering what to do. Then they scrambled to follow. They felt for their weapons, scraped their chairs back—didn't look at one another as they staggered, at confused intervals, toward the half-open door.

They entered the hotel lobby, drawn by the sound toward the sea-facing wall, which was made entirely of glass. The sound took shape there on the horizon in an angry cloud of helicopters and low-flying planes. When Lota first saw them they were far enough away as to appear indistinct—less objects in themselves and more an overall pattern in the air. But even in the time it took her to cross the lobby, to press her face against the glass, the horizon line shifted, and the planes could be clearly discerned.

She wondered if there'd been some mistake. Of course they'd anticipated some resistance—an Ø Com security force, perhaps, a couple of envoys from the Empire—*but this*!

Lota glanced down toward the hotel's lawn and the street. Both were littered with the refuse of the night before. Bottles and junk food wrappers, a few trampled articles of clothing, shoes. A couple of stragglers—an old man and a middle-aged woman—tottered innocently together near the entrance to Josie's canteen.

The sun was just beginning to rise. It occurred to Lota as she watched it—a discrete semicircle emerging like a yellowed thumbnail above the waves—how odd it was that, as opposed to the vibrant mix of colours projected by the setting sun at the end of a day, the rising sun projected nothing—was marked only by a gradual disappearance of darkness, an almost imperceptible increase of light.

She looked at the planes, then at the fluttering T-shirts and candy wrappers discarded on the lawn, and tried to feel something, but could not. She didn't even feel hollow anymore. The drone was too loud—the planes too close and too low—to feel anything but their approach.

Baby Jane had her hands on the glass, was staring out at the planes. Mystique and Bruno were also nearby—talking together heatedly. Lota looked around for Mad Max—for Kurtz. The noise outside droned louder. Lota swung back in time to see the noses of the planes dip slightly as they continued their descent. A sort of visceral panic set in—a reflexive reaction rather than a genuine response. She leaned in toward Mystique, but too late. She was already moving toward the exit at a sort of trot.

"Where's Kurtz?" Lota shouted at Bruno.

He shook his head. It was not clear if he'd heard.

"Kurtz!" Lota yelled again. "Where's Kurtz? What's going on?"

But by now Bruno was also moving toward the exit, still shaking his head. "The cable!" he shouted over his shoulder. "She's gone to cut the cable!"

"What?" Lota screamed. She ran toward him. "What about Mercer? What about the code?" Cutting the cable had only ever been a threat—a bartering chip, a hypothetical last resort. It had never been presented as anything more than that.

Bruno half turned; he looked at Lota blankly—as if he really didn't understand. Then he plunged through the door.

Lota followed. Baby Jane was right behind her. "What about the rest of us?" Baby Jane yelled after Bruno. "What are the orders?"

There was a terrific roar as one of the planes passed directly overhead—then a moment of relief.

"Where is everyone?" Baby Jane continued to shout. "Where's Norma? And Mr. Joshua?"

Bruno turned to face Lota fully now—although still it wasn't clear if he'd actually heard. He slapped at his face, which was unnaturally pale.

"Our orders," Lota repeated.

Bruno shook his head. "There are no orders."

Lota was gripping the butt of her gun in one hand. It felt smooth, and solid.

"What do you mean?" shrieked Baby Jane. "What do you mean, *no orders*?"

Bruno was slapping at his face again—tugging at both ears. Lota pulled out her gun. She flipped it over once, twice, in her hands, then she put it away.

"You stay here," Bruno told them. "I'll check in at the station." He began to pick his way across the short lawn. Lota stared after him. She glanced at Baby Jane, who had her eyes closed tightly, leaning on her gun.

There must have been something about Baby Jane's face in that moment—in her expression, which Lota couldn't entirely read—that reminded Lota of her mother, because, for the first time since she'd heard the planes, she thought of her back in the village. Thought of her looking up at the planes, shaking her head, defiantly praising God.

Then she thought of her brother Marcus—who for all she knew was aboard one of those planes. And then of her other brother, Miles, and of her auntie G, who were not.

Lota bit her lip, hard enough to make it bleed, and tried very hard not to cry. She hadn't cried—hadn't *really cried*—since she was a child. Not since her mother had told her angrily one night that she couldn't change things just by knowing about them—or by wanting to. That she had to accept both the good and the bad.

Baby Jane had opened her eyes. She was gazing at Lota and her old lined face looked tired—but she didn't seem either frightened or sad.

Embarrassed, Lota winced. She began to pace back and forth along the short magnolia-lined wall that bordered the hotel drive, listening to the sound of the planes in the distance, diminished now to a low hum. As far as she could see in any direction, nothing stirred. Even the couple she'd spotted outside Josie's canteen had tottered away somewhere. She glanced back once—apologetically—at Baby Jane, but Baby Jane wasn't looking at her anymore. She was looking out—past the rough coral and scattered couch grass, the shuttered houses and the lead tree groves—toward the sea.

Everything looked as it had always looked, as far back as Lota could remember; nothing had changed. It was impossible, therefore, to imagine that at the other end of the island a dozen or more planes were preparing to land like a flock of angry birds. Lota tried to picture them descending but could not. They continued to hover, in her mind's eye, above the empty lots and fields around the outer station. Try as she might, she could not bring them down.

And yet . . . they were descending. At that very moment, as Lota tried and failed to picture it, they were descending. The future was descending. But in a misshapen, unanticipated, and completely unrecognizable form. In another moment, Kurtz would cut the wire and the island would—more or less virtually—disappear. Or perhaps it had been done already, the moment passed. Perhaps they'd already been plunged, together, into . . .

Into what?

Again Lota's imagination failed her. She followed Baby Jane's gaze toward the water. She saw that the sun had risen fully now, a complete circle. It hung suspended, just above the waves, casting against the crooked shoreline its limited glow.

AFTERWORD

Everywhere in the world where knowledge is being suppressed, knowledge that, if it were made known, would shatter our image of the world and force us to question ourselves—everywhere there *Heart of Darkness* is being enacted.

SVEN LINDQVIST, *Exterminate All the Brutes*

This book represents my own effort at exploring the way that Joseph Conrad's *Heart of Darkness* continues to be enacted in our everyday lives. It is an effort that began for me back in 2009, when I encountered an article, published in *The New York Review of Books*, that quoted the military expert John Pike as saying that the U.S. military's goal was "to run the planet from Guam and Diego Garcia by 2015."[1]

I was both fascinated and appalled by how clearly Pike was able and willing to articulate the way that modern imperialism has reversed the expansionist aims of the recent past while, at the same time, keeping them wholly intact. Pike declared that the United States' current strategy for controlling as much of the world as possible was "by holding, directly at least, as little terrain as possible." By 2015, according to Pike's prediction, both power and capital would become literally "utopian" (from the Greek, "not-place"). America would give up its claim on actual peoples and territories—but only apparently. By *becoming*—that is, rather than merely conquering—"the biggest, the most blank, so to speak"[2] space on the map, the U.S. could, Pike suggested, run the entire planet within, and as, what Giorgio Agamben has referred to as a "state of exception."[3]

By the time this book project was in full swing, 2015 had come and gone. It is written, therefore, as it could perhaps only be written, in a sort of timeless state, where the near future collides with both the present and the past. My goal was to explore the many questions and problems that arise when considering the legacies of cultural imperialism, otherwise known as modern-day global capitalism. This book is also, therefore, a book about the "logistics" of whiteness and the hidden elements and/or bodies that "the science of whiteness" endeavours to control. It seeks to expose the materialities we take for granted in the concepts and systems that structure and support our everyday lives—thereby calling attention to "the full entanglement" of our experience on this planet with what is both visible and invisible, with others, and with otherness.[4]

I believe it's our collective responsibility to think about this entanglement—and try to identify, and dismantle, the logistics by which *Heart of Darkness* continues to be enacted not only all around us but *by us*. It's our responsibility to ask ourselves: How can we recognize each other outside of these concepts and structures? How can we become aware of our own invisibilities and the invisibilities of others—especially when our own seemingly "innate" processes of self-awareness are what often stand in the way? How can we encounter "blank" or unknown spaces or ways of being without, consciously or unconsciously, seeking to conquer them? How can we escape prescribed narratives without simply reinscribing binaries? How can we acknowledge the hidden materialities—and the hidden costs—of abstract concepts like subjectivity or our "wireless" world? How, finally, can we imagine a future that does not run along the exact same lines as the past?

---

1. Jonathan Freedland, "A Black and Disgraceful Site," review of *Island of Shame: The Secret History of the U.S. Military Base on Diego Garcia*, by David Vine, *The New York Review of Books*, May 28, 2009, www.nybooks.com/issues/2009/05/28.

2. From Joseph Conrad's *Heart of Darkness*: "Now when I was a little chap I had a passion for maps. I would look for hours at South America, or Africa, or Australia, and lose myself in all the glories of exploration. At that time there were many blank spaces on the earth, and when I saw one that looked particularly inviting on a map (but they all look that)

I would put my finger on it and say, 'When I grow up I will go there.' The North Pole was one of these places, I remember. Well, I haven't been there yet, and shall not try now. The glamour's off. Other places were scattered about the hemispheres. I have been in some of them, and . . . well, we won't talk about that. But there was one yet—the biggest, the most blank, so to speak—that I had a hankering after.

"True, by this time it was not a blank space any more. It had got filled since my boyhood with rivers and lakes and names. It had ceased to be a blank space of delightful mystery—a white patch for a boy to dream gloriously over. It had become a place of darkness" (Chapter 1).

3. The "state of exception" described by Agamben is an expression of the essential paradox at the core of our modern concept of sovereignty. It is the blurring of inside and outside, life and law, the exception and the rule. "The paradox of sovereignty," writes Agamben, "consists in the fact the sovereign is, at the same time, outside and inside the juridical order." Giorgio Agamben, *Homo Sacer* (Stanford: Stanford UP, 1998), 17.

4. In an interview with Niccolò Cuppini and Mattia Frapporti, Stefano Harney states: "Logistics delivers humans, animals, energy, earthly materials to an end, to a point, the point of production. But this includes, crucially, the point of production of the settler, the production of the entrepreneur, the banker, the slave trader, and the investor." Logistics exists, in other words—in reaction to and defence against entanglement and indeterminacy—as a way of accounting "for what goes missing." It is, in this way, also "the science of loss, the science of . . . lost means, which is to say it will always be the white science and the science of being white." How, Harney asks, do we remain "radically open" amidst all this, amidst "the war against us waged by *logistical capitalism*"? His answer? By remaining "open to each other," by allowing ourselves "to explore the full entanglement of our lives together and our full entanglement of this love, pain, and joy with each other in and of the earth." Niccolò Cuppini and Mattia Frapporti, "Logistics Genealogies: A Dialogue with Stefano Harney," *Social Text 136* 36, no. 3 (September 2018): 99–100, 97, 109.

ACKNOWLEDGMENTS

Thank you to Julie Iromuanya, Samson Verma, John Melillo, Erin Wunker, Farid Matuk, Janet Shively, and Ragini Tharoor Srinivasan, who read this manuscript at various stages and offered me their invaluable insights and suggestions. Thank you also to my editor, Nicole Winstanley, for her guidance, and for her belief in this work, as well as to Deborah Sun de la Cruz, Shaun Oakey, Karen Alliston, Stephen Myers, and everyone at Penguin Random House Canada. Thank you also to my agent, Tracy Bohan, for her encouragement, and to John, again, for his patience, love, and tremendous support.

A NOTE ON SOURCES

Selected speeches and texts in this novel have been either inspired by or adapted from The United States Declaration of Independence (1776); "Manifesto of the Equals," by Sylvain Maréchal (France, 1796); Francisco Indalécio Madero's proclamation to the Mexican Army (1910); Antonio I. Villarreal's article "Mexican: Your Best Friend Is a Gun!" (1910); Oswald de Andrade's *Manifesto Antropófago* (1928); Hannah Arendt's *Origins of Totalitarianism* (1951); Jacques Soustelle's speech to the Algerian Assembly, Algeria (1955); the Caravelle Manifesto, Vietnam (1960); Jean-Luc Godard and Jean-Pierre Gorin's film *Letter to Jane* (1972); the Manifesto of the New Jewel Movement, Grenada (1973); James McTeigue's film *V for Vendetta* (2005); Zack Snyder's film *Man of Steel* (2013); and Christopher Reeve's speech at the Democratic National Convention (2016).

I am also indebted to feedback from Joshua Polachek, to Nicole Starosielski's *The Undersea Network* (Duke University Press, 2015) and to the research of the many scholars whose work is included in Setsu Shigematsu and Keith L. Camacho's edited collection *Militarized Currents: Toward a Decolonized Future in Asia and the Pacific* (University of Minnesota Press, 2010).